SPUR CLOSED IN
ON THE BANK ROBBERS...

Spur moved over to the edge of the wall. He removed his hat with his left hand, peered into the lobby and whipped back to safety.

The image crystallized in his brain. A gunman held a woman by her throat. She knelt, looking pleadingly up at the man as he aimed at her.

"Say good-bye, girl!"

Spur lunged past the wall and peeled off a shot, instantly lining up his first target. The second man turned as his partner reeled. Spur's hogleg sounded again.

Both men went down as he paused, staring at them. Blue smoke filled the air and the echoes of the twin explosions bounced around in the big building for several seconds. Neither gunman moved....

Also in the *Spur* Series:

SPUR #31

PORTLAND PUSSYCAT

DIRK FLETCHER

LEISURE BOOKS NEW YORK CITY

A LEISURE BOOK®

December 2005

Published by

Dorchester Publishing Co., Inc.
200 Madison Avenue
New York, NY 10016

Copyright © 1989 by Chet Cunningham/BookCrafters

ISBN 0-8439-2884-0

The name "Leisure Books" and the stylized "L" with design are trademarks of Dorchester Publishing Co., Inc.

Printed in the United States of America.

Visit us on the web at www.dorchesterpub.com.

PORTLAND PUSSYCAT

CHAPTER ONE

Sunlight slanted in through the windows as Alain DuLac mixed the oils on his palette, looking for the right shade of red. It just wasn't the same. The rustic city of Portland, Oregon, wasn't Paris. He couldn't even buy the proper paints, the only ones that he could work with. Six months in this frontier town had depressed him.

DuLac shook his head and dabbed more white onto the smudge of dark red that bled onto his palette. He mixed the two hues with the brush and stared at the unfinished canvas on the easel. If only he could be back in Paris!

The old melancholy oozed through him. That was impossible, he knew. He could never again walk along the Seine, visit the bakery, see his family and friends. That part of his life was over forever.

The short, unkempt man snorted. "Chin up," he

said in his newly acquired English. "You should be happy you got out in time."

He remembered returning home from the bank, seeing the *gendarmes* surrounding his studio, hurling his possessions into the street. Unnoticed in the confusion, DuLac had gone back to the bank, withdrew every cent he had and caught the first ship to America.

It had been nearly a year ago.

Satisfied with the new shade he'd created, he started feathering in the highlights of the girl's hair. He wanted to capture the memory of the way the sun had glinted across Rebecca's tresses. DuLac became absorbed by the image. It was nearly perfect, so real that those lips seemed to be trembling, so vivid that he expected the breasts he'd created with paint to be soft and warm.

He added each strand of hair singly and soon had to turn up the lamps in his studio/apartment. As he bent toward the window to close the shades, he looked out at the shabby buildings and the dark bulks of the ships bobbing at the wharves.

Soon enough he'd be out of this neighborhood. Soon the people of Portland would recognize his talent and flock to buy his paintings. Soon he'd be able to stop his other business and become an honest man.

And perhaps, someday. . . .

The pudgy man pulled at the ends of his moustache, his eyes misting and blurring the image on the canvas. Someday in the future, he might return to his beloved Paris.

Harsh pounding pulled him from his reverie. DuLac shook his head, set down his palette and brush and went to the door. Was it time already?

It was. He silently admitted the tall, distinguished looking man.

"So you did not change your mind, Cummings," DuLac said, bolting the door behind him.

The man's face was barely visible under his low hat and the high collar of his coat. "No. Of course not." Though the room wasn't cold, his visitor pulled his jacket tighter around his gaunt body.

The artist nodded and went to the table that lay next to the bedroom door. This was how he made most of his money, DuLac thought, but that didn't stop him from hating such interruptions.

"These are flawless. Absolutely flawless." He retrieved a small satchel which he'd hidden behind a stack of leather-bound art books that morning.

"Sure, friend. Sure," Cummings said.

DuLac walked toward the man holding the bundle. "The same price as before. Correct?" He held the package out of the man's reach.

Cummings smiled and produced ten one-dollar bills from his coat pocket. They were folded and fastened together with a gold money clip. "You haven't reconsidered my offer, have you, DuLac? We could work real good together—your talent and my brains."

DuLac bristled. Always the same talk. "No. I am in business by myself and for myself. I do not need or want a partner." Cummings never changed. "I am a busy man. Are you going to buy or not?"

"Yes. Of course. But not at that price." He extracted half of the ones. "Five should do."

DuLac fumed and returned to the table. "No. One on ten. That is the way it is and will be."

"Not as far as I'm concerned."

The artist faced the enemy. "You think I am an

ignorant immigrant? That you can take advantage of me?"

Cummings smiled and stuffed the money into his coat pocket. "I think this is getting too dangerous for me. People are noticing. It's getting harder to pass your shit."

"This is the best that you can find!" DuLac puffed out his chest.

"Shut up!" Cummings' voice was harsh. "I'll give you five dollars for a hundred. Take it or leave it. But if you turn me down, you'll have visitors here, DuLac. Visitors in blue uniforms who'll be very interested in this business of yours."

"You dare to threaten me?" He walked to his easel, furious. "You are just as guilty as I, Cummings. In as much danger."

"I only passed it, friend. I didn't print it. I'm not the counterfeiter."

DuLac's fingers clasped around the wooden handle. "I am an artist! Get out of my studio!"

He heard Cummings approaching him from behind.

"Not until I get what I came for."

Now, he thought. The Frenchman extracted the long-bladed knife he'd hidden behind the easel and spun. Cummings didn't flinch as he continued toward the table.

"You won't use that thing on me, DuLac! You're no murderer!" He sneered, walked past the artist and pushed away the stack of books.

"You underestimate me!"

DuLac moved to him. Cummings had turned his back. A stupid mistake, the artist thought. He gripped the handle and brought it down, sheathing the steel. Cummings cried out as DuLac opened up his back.

The doomed man thrashed and dropped to the table. It was hard going at first, working the blade through flesh and gristle and the bones of his spine. DuLac gasped. Acidic sweat dripped from his brow. The short man stabbed Cummings ten times, caught up in the rage and passion, ripping up his back.

He raised the knife again and stared down. Cummings slumped over the table, unmoving, his arms dangling over its side.

Dead. He was dead.

A sickening smell filled the air, blotting out the comforting sweetness of the oil paints. DuLac wiped his forehead and breathed deeply, glancing around to see that all the shades were, indeed, drawn.

They were. He wiped the knife on a paint-splattered rag and threw it into the fireplace. It would serve as kindling that night. Now what to do with the body?

DuLac sighed. Counterfeiting. It always led to the same thing, to this uncomfortable feeling of having something to get rid of. He gripped the face-down man's waist and tried to heave him from the table. The body moved sideways and spilled onto the floor.

The artist panted.

A door opened. DuLac spun around, fear coursing though him, and smiled when he saw her step out from the bedroom. The red-haired young girl yawned and stood on shaky legs.

"You woke me up," she said.

"Rebecca, I—will you—"

She noticed the motionless form on the floor and

sneered. "Oh, Alain! Again?" The girl shook her head and sighed. "I suppose you want me to clean up the mess."

DuLac's shoulder ached. He walked to her, arms outstretched. "Please, my love, will you help me?"

She sighed. "Alright. Just like before. I'll get my friends to come over and take *it* away." Rebecca pouted. "But this is the last time, Alain! I mean it! You can't go around killing every man who argues with you. It's—it's messy!"

"You don't know what he was doing."

She tossed her head. "I don't care what he was doing." The girl fixed her eyes on his. "But Alain, if I do this, promise that I won't have to model for you again."

"Rebecca!" DuLac shook his head. He didn't want to lose her. "Look at the easel! Look at the work of art I created with your face!"

She glanced at it. Her face, with cascading red hair, remained cool. "Sure, it's pretty, but I'm bored sitting for hours and hours every day when I could be sleeping, we could be pleasuring each other or I could be smoking opium. I'm so tired of it, Alain! I can't do it again!"

"Okay. Alright!" He threw up his hands, tempering his anger with relief. "Just get your friends in here. I will find another model."

"Fine." Rebecca yawned and stretched. Her lovely form appeared beneath the loose robe.

DuLac stared at the seventeen year-old girl. The danger of the last few minutes transmuted to lust. He stepped over the body. "Get your friends later, okay?"

Rebecca smirked at him. "Sure. But don't try to

pay them with those phony twenty dollar bills of yours. Alain, give them real money. Okay?"

"Yes." He unbuttoned his pants. "And I'll give you this."

CHAPTER TWO

"Git on your belly or you're dead!"

The voice blasted at him as Spur McCoy entered the Portland Home Bank.

"I said move!"

Three rifle-toting men aimed at him. Tense people lay strewn all over the polished marble floor—tellers, little old ladies, grown men. The air was thick with the smell of fear.

Spur sighed. He'd walked right into a bank robbery.

"Now!" one of the gunmen shouted.

"Okay. Okay! I'm unarmed!" he lied and dropped to the floor.

Spur laid his cheek against the tile and turned his head, keeping an eye on things. One man stood guard as the other two forced the bank president to open the old-fashioned iron safe. He couldn't hear their words over the sniffles of the women sprawled around him.

"It'll be okay," he said to the girl lying a few feet from him.

"Shut up! No talking!"

She hesitantly smiled, clutching the beaded purse with her white knuckles.

Great. Just what he needed. He was in Portland to investigate the flood of counterfeit money that had invaded the monetary system and he ended up in this.

Spur was at least 20 feet from the closest guard, 30 feet from the other men and the safe. These men were professionals. No quirky movements, no hesitations. They acted as if they'd done this kind of thing before.

A lot.

"Hurry up!"

McCoy heard a metallic click. The safe must have been opened. The nearest guard turned to look at it for a second. Spur slid his arm down to the holster hidden under his coat tails.

He froze when the man wearing the kerchief snapped back, his full attention trained on his captives.

"Shit! That's all you got?"

The Secret Service agent bided his time, waiting for the right moment. A breeze swept in through the open windows. It slid over oak filing cabinets and bannisters and the tellers' windows, spreading fine dust throughout the bank.

"Come on! Empty it out!"

The guard scratched his nose. He raised his head.

"Uh. Uh. Uhhh!"

Spur drew his weapon, the action hidden from the guard by his leg. He slipped the revolver onto the cold floor, fingers tensed around its handle.

Wouldn't he ever sneeze?

"Uh. Oh hell!" the guard said, waving his own weapon through the dust-laden air.

He snorted. His nose exploded.

In that blinding second Spur slid to his knees and blasted hot lead into the guard's chest.

Without even checking to see if his ammunition had hit its mark, he dove for cover into the office cubicle that lay behind him.

"What in hell!" a voice said as the explosion echoed through the room.

Women screamed.

Spur waited.

"Damn! Andy's dead!"

"Who the hell did that!" It was the leader again. "Who the hell did it?"

Spur's muscles tensed as he crouched, kissing the wood with his shoulder. The walls were six feet high, tall enough to keep most men from looking over it. Because it was walled in on three sides, he'd have a clean shot at anyone who investigated.

"Didn't anyone see anything?"

"No!" the hostages chanted. A girl screamed and somewhere a baby cried.

Spur sweated.

"Then we'll just start killing you off one at a time until you remember! Who'll go first. You, sweetheart?"

They'd do it, Spur thought. They were professional thieves. He tightened his grip, his trigger finger itching to pull, to drive those bastards into the dirt.

He couldn't see. He had no idea what was happening. Time to take a chance.

Spur moved over to the edge of the wall. He

removed his hat with his left hand, peered into the lobby and whipped back to safety.

The image crystallized in his brain. A gunman held a woman by her throat. She knelt, looking pleadingly up at the man as he aimed at her.

The other thief walked among the people, throwing up coats, looking for weapons. They must have forgotten about him.

"Say goodbye, girl!"

Spur lunged past the wall and peeled off a shot, instantly lining up his first target. The second man turned as his partner reeled. Spur's hogleg sounded again.

Both men went down as he paused, staring at them. Blue smoke filled the air and the echoes of the twin explosions bounced around in the big building for several seconds. Neither gunman moved.

Spur McCoy stood, stretched his legs and walked fully into the open. The hostages started to sit up.

"I'd stay down for a while if I were you," he warned them. "They might not be dead."

He cautiously approached the second gunman and kicked his foot. Nothing. Spur peeled the fingers from the man's revolver and moved to the third man.

The leader lay face up. His kerchief, whipped partially away, showed a lifeless face. No breath issued from his parted lips.

Lucky shots, Spur thought as he collected another revolver. He checked both men's pulses just to be sure. They'd never rob another bank.

"Okay. It's safe now."

Fifteen souls rose. Grown men and women ran outside without even looking at him. The young girl who'd been at the other end of a barrel smiled and pressed his hand as she made her way out.

In seconds he was alone with three bodies and the bank president, who was busily stuffing the currency into the safe.

"I don't know who the hell you are, but I'm glad you stopped by today."

Spur nodded.

Dan Norcross sighed as he slammed the safe's door shut and rotated the tumblers. A tight-faced young man, a teller, had the conscience to return.

"Mr. Norcross?" McCoy asked.

"Go get Commissioner Golden!"

"Yessir!"

"Look, Norcross, I came here to ask you about the counterfeit money."

"Counterfeit?" Norcross scratched his head, his eyes dazed. "Oh yeah! Lots of that. Some of it's turned up here. Don't have a clue who's doing it." The ruddy-complexioned man blew out his breath. "I'm sorry. It's a little hard talking about that after all that's happened here." He surveyed the dead men and shook his head.

Spur nodded. "I understand. I'll stop by later."

When Police Commissioner Golden arrived at the bank, Spur quickly cleared up his involvement in the incident. Unwilling to discuss his secret Service mission in public, Spur arranged to meet him that afternoon in his office.

Now, outside, he took long breaths and strode along the street, admiring Portland's crisp air and beautiful buildings. He hadn't been in the Northwest for some time.

Spur re-read the telegram that his boss, General Halleck, had sent him from Washington. Jessica Gerard was the woman's name. He went to the address—305 Hudson Drive.

It was a small, dark shop full of crates, completely unsuitable for a woman. But as Spur McCoy walked inside his nose was filled with the scent of flowers.

The figure bending over the counter raised its torso and Spur smiled at the woman.

"Yes?" she wiped her gloves on the leather apron that covered her gingham dress. "Can I help you?"

She was in her mid-thirties, pretty, with penetrating eyes and a full, sensuous mouth.

"You're Miss Gerard?"

The woman pleasantly shook her head. "Mrs. Gerard. I'm widowed. Inherited this business from my husband when he passed on two years ago."

Spur nodded and walked up to the counter where piles of red and white roses lay. She'd been stripping off their thorns and throwing them into a coffee can.

"Spur McCoy. I understand you got some counterfeit money recently."

Her nostrils flared at the word. "Darn tooting!" Jessica pulled off the leather gloves revealing white, flawless hands. "It was in payment for wedding flowers. Can you believe that?" She chuckled. "When I took my cash to the bank that afternoon they informed me that they couldn't accept counterfeit money. I was shocked!" She laid a hand on her breast. "But old Edward Bidwell knows me. He told me to talk to the Commissioner. That's about it." Jessica looked at him, eyebrows raised.

"Who gave you this money?"

She reached behind her back and tried to unfasten the apron. "Heck. Could you help me with this?" The woman turned around and looked at him over her shoulder.

"Of course." Spur untied the straps and she struggled out of it, letting the heavy garment drop to the leaf-strewn floor.

"Thanks." Mrs. Gerard smoothed down the bodice of her brown, well-fitting dress. "It was the McInallys. Two old Scottish people. Said they met here and decided to get married three days later. They're on their honeymoon now—Geneva, I think." Jessica shook her head. "So I'm out my $20."

"They didn't look like the type of folks who'd print up their own money, did they?"

"No. Just plain people in love." She made a face. "I don't even remember what it's like to be that much in love."

He nodded toward the pretty woman. "Is there anything else you can tell me? I'm working with Commissioner Golden on the matter of the counterfeit money."

"I see." She narrowed her eyes and thought. "I'm sorry. That about it."

Spur nodded. The scent of roses in the close room was overpowering. As much as he enjoyed looking at the healthy woman, he had to get some fresh air. "How do you stand it?"

"What?"

"Well, Mrs. Gerard, flowers are fine, but this place smells like—like—"

Jessica smiled, flashing perfect white teeth at him. "A cheap whore?"

"Ah, yeah!"

"I'm not cheap, and I'm certainly not a whore. Oh Mr. McCoy, I don't even notice it anymore. I've been around them too long, I guess."

"That makes sense. If you think of anything else,

I'm staying at the Riverside Hotel."

"Fine."

"Good day, Mrs. Gerard."

"Good day, Mr. McCoy." Her hand went to her breast. "I—I hope I'll be seeing you again."

He hesitated before turning toward the door. Their eyes locked. "You can be counting on it."

McCoy heard her humming as he walked outside.

A half hour later, after he'd eaten in the hotel dining room, Spur returned to the bank.

"Mr. McCoy!" Dan Norcross said, rushing out of his chair to meet him. He took Spur's hand and pumped it up and down, squeezing his forearm. "I cannot tell you how happy I am that you dropped in earlier today." The bank president grinned at him.

"All in a day's work." He gently tried to take back his hand.

"Maybe for you, but not for me!" Norcross vigorously shook Spur's hand. "It was a nightmare until you started shooting. They had me by the balls!"

"Ah, Mr. Norcross," Spur said.

"Huh?" He looked down at their still-locked paws. "Oh. Sorry." The man released Spur's hand. "I'm just so—so grateful to you. We would have been ruined—not to mention what would have happened to the depositors and the poor, sweet girl who nearly got herself killed." He shuddered at the memories.

"Hey, relax, Norcross!" Spur said, flexing his hand. "That's in the past. Now what can you tell me about this counterfeit money that's been coming into town?"

"Huh? Oh, yes. Have a seat, Mr. McCoy." He

motioned to the well-worn chair in front of his desk. "It's good. Damn good. Finest engraving work I've ever seen." Norcross shrugged. "Of course, it doesn't hold up under close inspection. The printing's off and the ink and paper just don't match the real thing."

"Do you have any idea how long it's been passed here in Portland?"

"Hard to say." The bank president sucked in his cheeks and mulled it over. "I don't know. It could have been floating around for weeks or months before we caught on."

"That's understandable. It's normal not to be too careful until the word has gotten out. Do you have any of the counterfeit money here that I could take a look at?"

"I hope to hell I don't" Norcross laughed. "Sorry, I hauled it all over to the police commissioner's office. On Golden's orders I had my boys go through our funds. Found maybe, oh, ten or eleven of them. Not too bad."

"And how many other banks are in town?"

The president hummed for a moment. "You're talking about my competition. There are two official ones. First Oregon over on Adams and Grayson's Family Bank down by the river."

"Thanks for your time, Norcross. I better head over to Commissioner Golden's office."

The man rose with Spur. "Hey, the pleasure's been all mine!" His face beamed.

Spur started to extend his hand and drew it back, smiling. "Yeah, right."

CHAPTER THREE

"Get that corpse outta here!" a male voice barked from inside the office.

"Golden?" Spur yelled into the office. He darted around the two policemen carrying a sheet-wrapped body out of the wood-panelled room.

No answer.

He walked in. "Commissioner Golden?"

"Yeah. You look familiar." The bearded man glanced at him and sat on the edge of his desk, biting off the end of a fat cigar. "Weren't you at that robbery this morning?"

Spur nodded. "McCoy's the name."

"Sure! I gotta wire about you." He turned around and surveyed his paper-strewn desktop. "Somewhere. You must be from the Secret Service, the man the government sent out here about that counterfeit money."

McCoy closed the door. "Hope you don't mind, but I have to take precautions."

"What? No. I understand. I just can't find my damned matches!"

Spur smiled. "Look under your butt."

"What'd you say to me?"

"You're sitting on them, Golden. I noticed them as I came in."

The man stood, turned around and grabbed the matches. "You've got a good eye, McCoy. And you do some pretty fancy shooting."

Thanks. But I'm not in town to catch the kind of men who rob banks." He walked toward the desk. "I'm here about the counterfeit money."

"I know, I know." He struck a lucifer and held it to the end of the leaf-wrapped cigar, puffing until the fire took hold and the tip glowed. "All this bad money. Just what I don't need."

The man wasn't being very helpful, Spur thought as he tapped his right boot toe. Golden seemed bored.

"Do you have any information for me? Any leads, suspicious characters, some guy who's done this kind of thing here before?"

He shook his head. "No."

"What about that dead man?" Spur asked.

Golden snorted and blew out blue smoke. "If he was the counterfeiter, he won't be giving us any more trouble."

The veins in Spur's neck tightened. "Do you think there could be a connection between that man's death and the counterfeit money?"

"How in hell should I know?" Golden took aim at a brass spitton and hit it dead center. "Goddamn it!"

"Found a lot of bodies lately?"

"Yeah. We're dragging up about one a week. More than average, even for a place of this size. Things weren't looking so dead until recently—very recently." He grinned at his own joke.

The man grated on him. "Would you say the murders started about the time the fake money showed up?"

Golden was silent. He puffed, smiled and exhaled. "Hard to say. Maybe."

"And all the victims were men?"

"Yup. Stabbed, most of them. One shot through the heart at close range. Found them floating in the river. Five so far, including that last joker. No papers, no clothes, nothing to identify them."

"What are your instincts?"

"My what?"

Spur made a fist and banged it against his right thigh. "What are your feelings? Could the murders themselves be connected? Were they all done by the same man?"

"How the hell should I know?" Golden huffed and walked to the window. "The mayor's breathing down my neck about this, and the phony twenty-dollar bills aren't helping any. Lots of stores are refusing to take anything except a one dollar bill—or gold. I'm just praying someone doesn't set up his own mint in this town."

"Yeah."

This wasn't getting him anywhere. Golden was obviously the kind of man who sat behind a desk and dictated letters. He obviously didn't like to get his hands dirty. "Heard anything about any new arrivals in town causing trouble? Artists, maybe?"

Golden scowled. "McCoy, I don't look at pictures.

I'd rather play a good game of chess or enjoy a fine cigar." He took several puffs. "Of course, there is one type of fine art I enjoy." He went to the front of his desk, slid open a drawer and showed Spur a small painting of a nude girl. "Mighty fine brush-work there, eh? I don't know anything about art, but that gal's talented." He guffawed.

"Sure." The quality of the image was excellent. So good, Spur figured he'd be able to recognize the woman on the street. "Is it by a local artist?"

"Who the hell knows?" He slapped the painting into the drawer and banged it shut. "I can't read the artist's signature. Friend of mine picked it up for me—actually, I won it in a poker game last week."

Spur made motions to leave. "I'll check back with you if I turn up anything important."

"Yeah, I guess so. And if you meet any more dead bodies in the hall, tell them not to come in here!"

He shook his head and walked outside.

Artists, McCoy thought as his heels clicked on the floor. Wasn't there an artists' colony of sorts in town? He vaguely remembered passing a row of studios not far from the police station.

Five minutes later he found them. The squat, ill-kept cottages were hard by a two-story structure. "Portland Museum of Fine Arts," the sign said.

He walked in past a snoring security guard. A matronly woman accepted his dollar 'donation' with a smile. The rooms were filled with smoke, large and small canvases hung lopsided on the walls.

Not many people roamed the aisles. Those who were present were mostly older, well-moneyed couples with plenty of free time and not much to do. Spur passed a Renoir, a sketch by da Vinci and a Rembrandt before finding a small room labelled "Local Artists."

It was dimly lit. He pretended to study the paintings but was actually memorizing the names of the various painters. Laleque. Feingold. Bohannan. Johnson. Douglas. DuLac. Frantz. Weinholtz. And Emily Curtis—the only woman represented. Not surprisingly, the subjects of her paintings all seemed to be male.

"Don't you just love her work?" a feminine voice said at close range.

He turned and smiled at the young woman. "Ah, I'm not familiar with it." He tipped his hat.

"I'm not either." She peered at the painting. "But there's something about that man's face, something that makes me. . . ." The brunette shook her head. "I don't know." She self-consciously patted her hair. "I hope you don't think I'm, well—well—"

"What is it?" Something about the woman got his curiosity.

She sighed and looked up. "I'm not wearing a bonnet!"

"So I noticed." Spur liked the woman. "You have lovely hair."

"That's not the point!" Her voice was violent. "You know there's only one kind of woman who goes out without wearing a hat."

"I'm sorry." Spur was perplexed. "Is there something I can help you with?"

She clasped her hands. "I don't know. I'm so confused. Oh, I forgot to introduce myself. I'm Clare Maxwell."

"Spur McCoy."

"Nice to meet you, though I wish it were under different circumstances." She frowned, marring her natural beauty. "I was nearly thrown in jail this morning—and not for what you may be thinking."

"I'm not thinking that."

"All I did was try to buy a new hat, and the sweet-faced lady grabbed my arms! She wouldn't let go and started screaming to her husband!"

"Let me guess. Did you try to pay with a twenty dollar bill?"

Clare widened her eyes and smiled. "Yes. How'd you know?"

He shrugged. "There's a lot of that going around. You must be new in town."

"That's right. Just got in two days ago from San Francisco."

"Where'd you get the bill?"

She looked away from him. "I'd—I'd rather not tell you that."

Over her shoulder Spur saw her left cheek redden. Spur smiled at her. The woman turned and started to speak, but he took her hand.

"I'm *not* thinking that, believe me! It's none of my business anyway."

Clare hung her head. "Alright. Go ahead. Call me a saloon girl, a tart like my mother used to say. But I'm not the whore of Babylon!"

"Fine." He'd never met a woman like her. Ever. She was obviously educated, well-fed, healthy and full of life. But she didn't have the money to buy a hat?

"I should be going. I have to earn some more—I mean, I—" Her blush deepened.

"Miss Maxwell, it's no concern of mine what you do. Honestly."

She shook her head. "Anyway, I really do like Emily Curtis's paintings."

The woman looked at him, flinched and ran off.

Spur watched the woman's hips swaying back and forth. He hoped her next customer would give her clean money produced by the United States Bureau of Engraving and Printing.

Until sundown, Spur poked through the artists' studios, gently asking questions, trying to root out any suspicious remarks from the motley assortment of individuals who did indeed fit the artistic temperament. He even visited Emily Curtis for a few moments. The artist turned out to be an eighty-year-old cigar-smoking gal who liked her male models more than selling her paintings.

Nothing.

A whore!

At least I have a bonnet for this outfit, Clare Maxwell thought as she struggled into the stiff black dress. She used her black handkerchief to scrape a layer of dust from the hotel room's cracked mirror and pinned the dark hat on her head. Lowering the veil to cover her face, she bent her torso forward, drooped her chin and grabbed the cane.

She looked perfect. No would suspect the woman inside the clothes was twenty-two years old.

Gleeful and excited as she always was, she pressed an ear to the door and listened. Footsteps and soft laughter in the hallway outside. She waited until all was silent and slipped out of her room.

As she slowly, slowly made her way to her favorite spot, Clare realized that she had to be careful. True, she didn't think she was in any danger of the police. Who would bother an old lady? Still, the counterfeit money she'd gotten yesterday had shaken her. What was the point if all she took home was pieces of paper that no bank or shopkeeper would accept?

An hour until sunset. She walked to the corner, pretending to measure every step she took, leaning heavily on the cane, and started crying. At least, she hoped it sounded like crying.

Clare Maxwell finally paused in the middle of a block near the milliner's store where she'd been rebuffed earlier that day. A likely candidate walked toward her.

She put her act into overdrive, sobbing, reeling, pretending to lose her balance. She dropped the cane and wailed just as the young woman passed her.

"What is it?" the girl asked.

"No. No. No one cares about an old lady!" Clare glanced up at her, hunched over. From behind her veil the girl looked fresh-faced, well-dressed and just of marrying age.

"You poor dear. Come on, tell me!"

She panted. "Could—could I borrow a handkerchief?" she asked, sniffling.

"Of course." The girl opened her purse and handed her a lacey square of linen.

Clare took it and deepened the crackle in her voice. "Oh, I've dropped my cane." She stumbled forward.

"Here, let me get that for you."

Clare got into position as the girl bent over. In seconds flat she retrieved her cane, grabbed the purse and ran like hell down the street.

"Hey!"

Jubilant, Clare raced along the sidewalk, her black dress flying. She shoved the purse down her bodice, wedging it between her large breasts and laughing.

The girl had looked wealthy. If so, now Clare Maxwell was happy to have gotten a share of it.

She prayed that she didn't find any more counterfeit money.

CHAPTER FOUR

Spur spent much of the night curled up under a flowerbox across the street from the small artists' colony. Though it was spring, the air blowing off the Williamette River was chilled. He watched the small, squat cottages, waiting for something suspicious to happen, but had seen nothing more unusual than young women of questionable virtue (but obvious talent, as the police commissioner would say) slipping into the small structures.

If there was a counterfeiter among the artists, he certainly wasn't showing his hand. Spur chuckled into the collar of his coat as not one but two strapping men boldly walked into Emily Curtis's place. They didn't leave for nearly two hours. This was a little late to be painting, he thought with a wry smile, trying to picture the elderly woman tangled up with the bucks.

After sitting there half the night, wrapped in shadows, he returned to his hotel and tumbled into bed well after midnight.

McCoy didn't wake until eight. Walking to the windows to let in blinding sunlight, he wondered what his next moves would be. He had no leads whatsoever.

As he scraped off his whiskers with cold water and a semi-rusty blade, Spur realized that even if a working artist had gone into the money-printing business, he probably wouldn't have the operation set up in his studio. Naturally, not all the artists in Portland were located on that one street. A few of them must have made a fortune and had built fine homes.

He shook his head and splashed fresh water onto his face from the pitcher. What would he do? Track down every artist in town, break into their homes and search them?

Spur smiled at his misty reflection, wiped off his face and answered the urgent knock that suddenly issued from his hotel room door.

A bespectacled boy thrust a folded piece of paper to him and held out his hand. Still groggy, he handed the kid a quarter and slammed the door shut.

Another telegram from General Halleck. As always, Spur had wired his hotel and room number to his boss. What was it this time?

Bare chested, he sat on the bed and read. The man who'd transcribed the message wrote in a clean, neat hand, something which he hadn't encountered very often in the ruder towns of the west.

His boss had given him a new assignment while he was in the area. He was to investigate some sort of slavery operation located somewhere outside of Portland. A logging and sawmill business. The owners have been importing males from the Hawaiian Islands and forcing them to work sixteen hours a day under the most grueling conditions, felling trees and sawing lumber under armed guard.

The men are underfed, unpaid and unable to leave. Ankle chains. Beatings. Those who died were quickly replaced by fresh human stock. One man had managed to escape with a bullet in his stomach and told this to a passing sheriff before he'd died.

He'd been given the assignment because the slaves had been transported from Hawaii to the state of Oregon.

Spur frowned. He didn't need this diversion, but he'd be glad to crush it out of existence. The thought of men doing things like that to other human beings made his skin crawl. He carefully reread the telegram, deciphered its code, but it contained no indications of where the operation was located.

His mind raced. A sawmill? They had to sell lumber. Maybe excess logs. Who's buying, and did they know or care where the merchandise was coming from? Maybe the low prices that kind of labor could produce halted any questions.

It had to be located on the water to quickly move the lumber. A river, probably. It must be an armed, rigidly-run camp secreted somewhere in the woods. There wouldn't be open trails blazing toward it. On the water the men in charge could go to and from the camp by boat. It all seemed reasonable.

Spur pulled on his boots and dressed. He'd spend the rest of the day working on the counterfeiters and set out first thing in the morning to look for the outlaw logging operation.

He was getting tired of this city life, he thought, pushing the low-brimmed Stetson on his head. It'd feel good to get back on a horse again.

"Wake up!"

Groggy from his nap, DuLac growled as the young girl shook his shoulders. "Why? Are you going to spread your legs for me?" He lazily grabbed Rebecca's thigh.

"No! Not now!" Her hand brushed his away.

He rolled over. "Then let me sleep."

"Come on, Alain! We have to talk!"

The artist sighed and rubbed his face. "Why are you young girls so—so energetic all the time?"

"You never complained before."

DuLac sighed and sat up. "Alright." He kissed Rebecca Ledet's cheek. "What is it?"

She backed away from him, pouting. "I was robbed!"

DuLac regarded her with sleepy eyes. "I see."

"Robbed. Right on the street, during the day!"

"So. Did you have any real money in your purse?"

"Sure. fifteen dollars." The seventeen year-old girl smiled. "I managed to get change for one of your bills."

He waved a finger at her. "See? I keep telling you that I am a good engraver!"

Rebecca rolled her eyes. "Don't start that again! That's not the point. I mean, all I did was stop to help this old lady who was crying her eyes out. The next thing I knew she'd grabbed my purse and was flying down the sidewalk like—like some witch on a broomstick!"

"My dear, you exaggerate."

"No! Alain, I—"

"Please, Rebecca. I can replace whatever you lost. You know that. If this is your clever way to get more money from me, you do not have to be so elaborate."

"It's not that. Besides, Alain, it's getting harder and harder to find anyone in town who'll take a twenty dollar bill. Your *artwork* is worrying lots of people. And that worries me. What'll happen to us if we have to live on the sales of your paintings?"

The immigrant winced. "Please, girl. They will see my talent. Soon I will have a big exhibition in the museum. I can buy you anything you want with real money."

She snickered. "Not if you're locked up."

DuLac shook his head. "How would anyone find me? I am safe. We are safe."

Rebecca stroked his chest hairs. "I know, but I think you should stop—"

"No."

"—stop selling for a while."

"No!" He blinked. "Do not say that!"

He heard her gasp. "Alain, darling, I don't want to leave you."

DuLac frowned. Here it comes, he thought. His young model, the girl he'd shared his bed with for the last month, who'd spent all his money, was turning her back on him. He rubbed his eyes and took the girl's hands in his. "You forget where you were when I found you."

Rebecca looked stubbornly at the ceiling.

"You were common, a cheap whore, selling your virtue on the streets."

"I didn't sell my virtue. I sold myself. And I got a good price too!"

"Rebecca, listen to me. Everything is fine. I will stop printing as soon as I can afford to. Until then—take the money on the dresser."

She licked her lips. "How much?"

"Thirty dollars—real money."

"Oh, Alain!" Rebecca kissed his forehead. "You're such a dear man."

"Do not forget it," he said, grunting.

The girl snuggled up beside him. "How can I ever repay you?"

DuLac felt the old desires rising up in him.

The two men faced each other in the downtown alley. Brick walls rose up on either side; garbage festered around their feet.

"Hey, you trying to rob me?" the dealer said. "This is the best! Look at it! Better than before. The paper's better. The ink's closer to the real thing!"

"Keep your voice down, Jameson! The deal's off. I'd have to go outside of Portland to spend it, and I don't need that kind of trouble." He started walking away.

"A twenty for three dollars."

"No."

"Two!"

The departing figure stopped. "Well. . . ."

Jameson pulled four more bills from his pocket. "I'll make you a deal. Take the whole bunch--a hundred dollars worth--for seven dollars. Shit, with that much money you could afford to make a little trip to Astoria or some other town. Whaddya say, guy?"

"What do I say?" The man smiled and reached into his coat pocket. "You're under arrest, stupid!"

"What--" Jameson bolted.

Counterfeit money flew through the air. The criminal raced past the officer, cursing.

"Don't—"

He fired. That was all he could do. Jameson darted a few more feet and crumpled to the bare ground, filling a puddle with his body.

The policeman approached him. Damn! All that work and he'd blown it. They'd never find out where Brian Jameson had gotten the counterfeit money now. He stormed back, gathered up the bills that lay strewn in the alley, safely tucked them into his pocket and hauled the body to the police station.

Golden wouldn't be glad to see him. He started thinking about getting into another line of work.

"Competition? I have no competition, Mr. McCoy. As the only lady artist with a following in Portland, I stand alone." Emily Curtis smiled pleasantly at him.

"I understand. Then you wouldn't mind talking about your fellow artists?"

She laughed throatily. "Dabblers. No professionals among them. I could paint rings around their work any day!" Emily leaned toward him and lowered her voice. "They don't have the calling, you see?"

McCoy nodded. She smelled of lavender and, curiously, of tobacco. "Do you know if any of them might be involved in, ah, unsavory activities?"

The white-haired woman tilted her head. "What are you getting at?"

"Confidentially?"

She nodded, her eyes sparkling. "Yes, yes, I understand all that. You have no idea how many secrets I've had to keep about my models."

Spur grinned and remembered the two men he'd seen entering her studio last night. "Counterfeiting."

Emily Curtis set her jaw, straightened the lace collar of her white dress and turned. "What do you think of that?" she said, pointing a bony finger at a half-finished portrait of a young man.

"Very nice. Excellent. Finishing the eyes will bring it to life."

The artist suddenly turned, her skirts swishing with the movement. She stared hard at him, studying him, summing up the man. "Mr. McCoy, I've heard nothing about such doings among those gentlemen. But if I do, I shall certainly inform you. Where can you be reached?"

It was his turn to size up the woman. Her straight back and pungent personality didn't rile him. On the contrary, she seemed a woman of her word. "The Riverside Hotel. Room 305."

"Fine." She brushed her hands together. "Have a pleasant afternoon."

Spur walked outside, hoping that Emily Curtis just might learn of something that could help him. He walked above the Williamette River, admiring the broad, flat expanse of water and various craft surging up it or riding gently along the current.

He was surprised to see a Chinese junk—aptly named, Spur thought—sailing along, its massive, ill-shaped sails filling with the stiff springtime breezes.

Unfortunately, he didn't see whatever he bumped into.

"Oh!" It was a high voice.

Spur grabbed the woman's shoulders and stepped back. "I'm terribly sorry, Mrs. Gerard!" he said as the businesswoman spilled two dozen white roses onto the ground.

"No, it's my fault, Spur. Darn it! Now I'll have to start all over again." She looked down at the dirty roses, then up at him. "I was enjoying watching the river, not minding where I was going."

"So was I."

Jessica Gerard was so vibrant, so fresh when out of her storefront business. The woman's blonde hair spilled out of her simple hat. Her impressive breasts strained against the thin material of her dress, threatening to burst it. Jessica laughed and kicked at the roses.

"I don't care about them, but the Riverside Hotel does. I have to get them another two dozen as soon as possible."

"The Riverside? That's my hotel."

"What a curious coincidence, Spur." Jessica tucked in a lock of hair that had fallen over her forehead.

"May I accompany you?"

"Of course."

He took her arm. Soon she had prepared 24 more roses and dropped them off at the front desk, where the manager assured her they were right on time for the honeymoon couple on the fourth floor.

They went to the hotel's front door. "Having to do all that work again has just tuckered me out. Spur, do you think I could have a short rest—in your room?"

Their gazes locked together for a moment. "Of course, Mrs. Gerard."

The manager smiled at them as they ascended the stairs. The woman plainly wasn't tired, for she bounded up the stairs like a little girl eager for a treat. Once inside his room Spur locked the door and turned to her.

Jessica unpinned her hat and threw it away. Glowing yellow ringlets cascaded to her shoulders. The beautiful woman writhed like a cat, staring hungrily at him.

"I want you!" she said with undisguised lust.

"I thought you wanted to rest." Spur went to her, feeling tremendous desire pulsating through his body.

"Yes. After we finish." Jessica Gerard motioned for him to hurry his steps, met him halfway and started fumbling with his belt.

"Hey! We're in no hurry, are we?" Spur asked, surprised at her eagerness.

"I am. Come on, Spur! It's been two years. Two long years since I had a man! You don't know what it's like." Her voice was breathy. "I think I'm entitled. Don't you?"

"No complaints from me!"

"Good." Her dextrous fingers managed to slip the end of the leather belt through the buckle. Jessica slid it from the loops around his pants.

Spur was surprised when the woman moved behind him. Her warm mouth pushed through the hair that hung over his neck, sought and found the tender flesh. He gasped as her warm tongue licked him.

"I like that."

She bit him, sending shivers up and down his spine. Spur reached for his fly but the woman's hands gently grabbed his wrists and urged them behind his back.

He sighed at the erotic contact, fidgeting, letting her do what she wanted. After all, she'd waited for this for such a long time.

Spur didn't lose his smile until he felt the woman tightening the belt around his wrists, fastening them together behind his back.

Tieing him up!

CHAPTER FIVE

"Hey!" Spur said, struggling against the wide leather belt that cut into his wrists.

"Now, now," Jessica Gerard said, tightening the loop.

In seconds, the woman had managed to bind his arms behind his back.

"Jessica, what are you doing? I thought we were going to—"

She laughed. "We are, big boy. Haven't you ever done it like this before?"

"No. Ah, no. And I don't feel very good about it right now."

She walked in front of him and gave him a tight-lipped smile. "You will."

"That belt's pretty tight. Did you used to be a policeman, too?"

Jessica laughed. "No. It's just that Horace—my

late husband—taught me to pleasure him the way he liked it." She unbuttoned her dress. "He was the only man who ever had me, so I don't know any other way. Doesn't every man and woman do this when they—do it?"

"Well, not really." Spur had to smile at her. "Come, on, Jessica untie me."

She stood demurely before him as she unfastened the last button and let her dress slip to the floor. Her luscious body was plainly visible under the silky chemise and single petticoat.

"You're beautiful, Jessica!" Spur said, stumbling toward the woman.

She backed away. "Uh-uh!"

"What?"

"No! Not until I say so."

Spur looked down at the bulge in his crotch. "*That* says so."

She followed his gaze and grinned as she ran her hands up her chest and cupped her breasts. "Do you want these?" Jessica asked, tilting her head back and staring at him from lowered eyes.

"Yes, God, yes!"

She gently pinched the hard nipples that stuck against her chemise. "How much do you want them?"

"Right now, more than anything else!" Spur struggled against the belt. The woman was driving him mad. The incredible beauty she was offering him, and his inability to enjoy it, infuriated him. The erection in his pants was painful.

Jessica smiled. "Do you want them more than having your arms free?"

"Yes. Jesus, Jessica, Yes!"

The young woman pressed her hands between her

legs, covering the triangle underneath her transparent petticoat. "And this? Is this what you want?"

"Come on, Jessica!" Spur said, gasping. Any second it would rip out the buttons in his fly.

She rubbed herself up and down, digging her fingers into the clinging material.

"You enjoy torturing me, don't you woman?"

Jessica sighed, shook her head and ran to him. "Hell, no!" In seconds she had his hands free.

He grabbed her shoulders, backed her to his bed and forced her to sit. "No more tricks, okay?"

She nodded.

Spur lifted his right boot. She expertly pulled it off and then freed his left foot. the Secret Service agent threw off his coat, shirt, pants and long underwear and gripped his erection.

"I don't have to ask you if you want this, right?"

The woman moaned, staring at it, biting her lower lip.

"Didn't think so." He slid off her chemise and tugged the petticoat from her lower body.

"Ahhhhh yes. Yes indeed, ma'am!"

Jessica put her arms around him. "Do it. Do anything you want, Spur!" she hissed. Jessica raised her feet to the edge of the bed, spreading her legs, opening herself to him.

He stroked his penis and briefly glanced at the belt. No. He wouldn't use it. "Okay."

He knelt. Jessica gasped as he licked her left nipple, flicking his tongue back and forth over the hard, pink mass of flesh. She was delicious, warm and sweet with a whisper of rose petals.

Spur switched and stuffed most of the other mound into his mouth. He nursed on her breast and gently teethed it. Low moans issued from Jessica's throat.

He was more than ready but he decided to slow things down—for him, that is. He let her breast slip out of his mouth and kissed the soft skin between them, then pecked and bit her flesh, moving his head downward, toward the blonde mystery that lay between her thighs.

As he neared it Jessica arched her back. Trembling hands gripped his ears as Spur pushed into her crotch. It was moist and hot. He licked the outer lips, savoring the healthy taste of the woman, teasing her as he inhaled her sex-musk. Jessica bucked and moved his head. The woman gasped and went into convulsions as he locked his teeth around her clitoris and sucked.

"Mmmmmm."

"Oh. What are you doing to me?" she said between gasps.

He made love to her with his mouth and tongue, flicking back and forth, sending her into spasms of pleasure. Spur was enjoying himself immensely but the firm flesh between his legs demanded attention.

"No!"

The word escaped from her as he lifted his head, but Jessica sighed as he rose. He pushed her onto her back and fit his body between her legs.

"Yes!"

Jessica's face was flushed and shiny. He was perfectly positioned. Everything was lined up.

Spur waited, rubbing the head of his penis along her opening, feeling the jolts of fire that ran between their bodies at the intimate contact. Jessica groaned, clasped her hands around his torso and pushed her hips forward.

Spur sighed. The hot, liquid contact increased as he slid into her an inch at a time, prolonging his penetration. He pushed his tongue into the woman's mouth. Their hips locked together; his scrotum pressed against her soft buttocks.

She felt so good, so warm and tight and willing. McCoy kissed her savagely and she took his tongue, gasping as their lips slammed together and he thrust into her mouth.

Slowly, slowly, he withdrew. The simple motion made her shudder. Jessica's hands trailed down his back and fastened onto his hips.

"Come on, Spur," she said, her voice dreamy and low with lust. "Come on! It's been so long!"

"Okay." He pushed into her full-length. Jessica smiled up at him, eyes wide, nostrils flaring.

He did it again. Her breasts bounced.

Again. Faster.

Spur pumped between the woman's legs, driving into her, connecting their bodies with his erection. Jessica laid back. She gazed up at him in innocent awe, her throat tightening with each thrust.

"Yes. Oh God, yes!"

He jabbed into her body with deep, manly strokes. Spur raised himself on his hands and rode her higher, ensuring that he stimulated the woman to even greater peaks of pleasure. Their bodies furiously rubbed together, shooting off sparks, heating them.

Spur's movements became faster, harder. She dug her fingernails into his hips and forced him even deeper into herself. Their bodies slapped together at the waist. Jessica's moans quickly matched Spur's and then trembled in intensity, rising as the woman slithered underneath him, mouth open, eyes widening until she shook and whimpered and gasped through the ultimate peak of pure, sexual sensation.

The woman's climax encouraged Spur. He kissed her again and slammed into her body, driving himself right up to the edge but not caring, blindly thrusting and bucking until the fantastic release washed through him. Every muscle in his sinewy body contracted. He plunged full-length into her, spasming and orgasming and spurting his seed into her body, grunting as the awesome sensations swept her up again. They clutched each other, fingers digging into flesh as pure pleasure exploded deep inside them.

Ecstasy flooded through him. Spur sighed and gently kissed her lips, slowly pumping, gasping around her tongue. Jessica softened her grip on his buttocks and sighed as their hearts raced in unison.

He plunged into her one last time and lifted his head, looking in amazement at the woman below him. Her eyes were misty, filled with all the things a woman felt at times like that.

It was too much. He collapsed on top of her and they rested, lying connected over the edge of the bed, satisfied, sated.

Later, hours later it seemed to him, Spur was aware that he was crushing the woman. He started to move, withdrawing his still swollen penis from her, but Jessica grabbed his waist to keep him on top of her.

"What do you think you're doing?"

"Aren't I too heavy for you?"

She laughed. "No. It feels good."

He pecked her chin and took her head in his hands.

"I—I can't believe it. I'd forgotten what it's like. Two years, Spur!" Her eyes sparkled.

"You sure haven't forgotten what to do."

"Just hold me, you big brute!"

Spur did.

Model wanted the sign in the window said. Clare Maxwell thought about it as she stood outside the artist's studio and shrugged. Her short career at larceny hadn't been too successful. All those counterfeit bills showing up. She'd seen so many, she could get a job at a bank spotting them.

The young woman sighed and shook her head. "Why not?" she asked herself and went in.

A short, pudgy, moustached man looked up at her.

"Yes?" he said. "You come here to buy paintings?"

"No." Something about his European accent comforted her. Such men were more—well, cultured. "I'm here about your sign in the window."

The artist squinted at her. "Huh? Oh, yes. You have come to model for me!"

"Right. If you'll take me."

"Hmmm." He set down his brush. "Move into the light. Come along, my dear. Nothing to be afraid of."

"I'm not afraid." Clare walked confidently to the postion he'd indicated, before the floor-to-ceiling windows that opened up to a walled-in garden.

"Turn around, please?"

She slowly swirled, remembering every poise lesson her mother had given her all those years ago.

"Yes. You will do nicely. You do realize that this is nude modeling, don't you, my dear?"

Clare smiled. "I figured as much."

"Does the thought of taking off your clothes in front of me bother you?"

She studied the man. The more she looked at him, the more he could be her father. "For modeling? No. Of course not."

"Splendid!"

"How much?"

"I beg your pardon?" He went to her.

Clare felt him analyze her form with his eyes. "How much will you pay me to model for you?"

The artist smiled. "Ten or twenty dollars, depending on how long you are willing to pose at one time. But it will never be longer than an hour."

Twenty dollars! Clare smiled. "Mister, you just got yourself a model!"

"Fine. Splendid!"

She allowed the funny man to take her hand and kiss it, European fashion. "When do we start? Right now?"

"Ah, no. I do not have time for a full session this afternoon." He mused, putting his paint-smeared hand on his chin. "Maybe a quick sketch, to see if we can work together?"

"Okay. What should I do?"

The artist smiled and tugged at his shirt sleeves. "Undress, please."

Clare sighed and did as she was told. At least it was better than trying to earn a living robbing women's purses. And safer too. Clare had no desire to spend a few years locked away in a jail cell.

She reached for the buttons on her dress. The artist thoughtfully turned his back on her, searching for a suitable sheet of art paper, rifling through the bottles of brushes. Clare swallowed hard and removed her clothing. After all, this was art, wasn't it? Art isn't a sin.

"The door," Clare suddenly said, glancing at it. "What if someone comes in?"

"Ah! Of course. I am used to working with another model who did not care. Forgive me."

He didn't even glance at her as he crossed the cluttered studio, locked the door, and began lowering all the shades save for those on the garden windows.

Clare giggled as she removed her petticoats. Now stark naked, firmly resolved to give up her life of crime, she felt strangely free. Smiling, she arched her back and pointed a toe. "Like this?"

The artist turned toward her. His face lit up with a smile. "Yes. Perfect! Your form is ideal." He grabbed a charcoal pencil and started sketching.

As he worked Clare relaxed and thought about her future, completely unconcerned by the man's presence in the room and her vulnerable condition. That artist wouldn't hurt a fly.

A door to her left—not the front door—suddenly banged open.

"Darling, can't you—oh, I'm sorry, dear!"

Clare smiled at the young woman who appeared in the studio. If it had been a man she would have covered herself, but faced with a member of the same sex, she just relaxed. After all, she was going to be immortalized—and get paid for it!

"Can you not see that I am working?" the artist shouted with sudden ferocity.

She winced. "It can wait." The young woman sneered at Clare and disappeared.

"Where was I?" the man said, pulling on the ends

of his straggly moustache.

Clare's smile froze as the girl's face impressed itself on her mind. She'd seen it before.

Of course there was no way the girl would recognize her. She'd worn the black old woman's outfit when she'd robbed her, and not long afterward had thrown the expensive purse into the river. But the unexpected sight of that face chilled her. She was thankful she'd stopped that dangerous hobby.

"Please. Clare, is it? Please relax. You are tensing up all over the place!"

"I'm sorry. I've never done this before."

"You will grow accustomed to it."

She pushed her shoulders back just enough and repositioned her right toe in front of her. Clare made a conscious effort to keep her arms loosely dangling at her sides as she thought. That girl must live with him. His daughter? No. Like most artists, he'd probably taken an unlawful lover.

Clare sighed, remembering how she'd returned to her hotel room and locked the door. She'd gleefully looked over the treasures she'd just obtained, only to find a counterfeit twenty dollar bill. At least the fifteen dollars in real money, plus a small silver dollar, had made up for her work.

"There. Done!" the artist said.

The man's words broke her reverie. "I can get dressed?"

"Yes. Please."

She hurried into her clothing. Once again the artist didn't look at her. He gave her complete privacy as if he wasn't interested in her as a woman. That suited her fine, Clare thought, buttoning up her dress.

When she was finished the man surprised her by pressing two dollar bills into her hand.

"What's this for?" she asked, fingering the money. It seemed to be genuine but she just couldn't trust anyone these days.

He smiled. "To ensure that you come back. Same time tomorrow afternoon?"

She nodded. "Yes. Fine."

He unlocked the front door for her. "Good day, Miss Maxwell."

Her skin was crawling as she stepped out of the studio. The door banged shut and she heard the click of the lock. Clare hadn't minded posing for him, and indeed it was kind of an honor to think she was worthy of being painted. But the close call with the girl had been scary.

She shook her head and blinked, allowing her eyes to adjust to the harsh sunlight. Well, wasn't that an experience, Clare thought. And she'd go back, even face the young girl, if it meant steady money coming in. Besides, she wanted to see herself in a painting.

Maybe he'd transform her into Diana, queen of the heavens, or Juno, or that sweet, tragic, Helen of Troy.

Clare realized that she didn't even know the artist's name. She looked up at the sign in the window: "A. DuLac, European Portrait Artist."

CHAPTER SIX

Spur McCoy's trip into the countryside the next morning led him through lush valleys, past sparkling streams and atop small hills. His rented horse was sure-footed and wasn't easily exhausted. McCoy didn't work the mare too hard, regularly stopping to allow the beast to forage and suck the sweet water that seemed to flow everywhere through this area outside of Portland.

After a few hours, Spur realized he wasn't going to just happen upon the illegal logging operation. He never expected to, but it sure would be a nice surprise.

McCoy searched for rivers large enough to float trees, for rude trails that might lead to the camp, or some hint that he might be near the place. But nothing showed itself.

He returned to the city in the early afternoon. Spur visited the Bar B Lumberyard, found the owner, and asked the hard-faced man where he bought his wood.

"Johnson's Mill and Steele's Timber," he said with hesitation. "They got offices right in town," the man with the handlebar moustache said. "Best prices around, too."

"Thanks."

Spur visited both cramped, dirty offices and talked with their representatives. They seemed perfectly legitimate. Another dead end.

He walked his horse back to the wharf. A medium sized ship was off-loading freshly sawed boards from its hold. Spur secured his horse and approached a bearded, shabbily-dressed man who stood with his arms crossed on his chest. He was apparently overseeing the operation.

"New wood?" Spur asked him.

"That's a fact." The man spat a brown glop of saliva onto the wooden flooring.

"I'm gonna put up five stores on Hudson Street," Spur said, spinning his tale. "Need lots of lumber. You know where I might buy me some cheap wood? I mean—below normal cost?"

The captain's left eyelid twitched as he sized up McCoy. "Why?"

"Want to save money."

"Don't we all!" He mused. "I won't ask you if I can trust you because no man's worthy of that." He stuffed another plug of tobacco into his jaw and sucked it. "Fact of the matter is, I do know."

Spur tempered his show of interest. "Where?"

"Damnit! Watch that load!" The captain motioned to his hired hands. "What was I saying? Oh yeah. Can't tell you much, but I can tell you this. Bend of a river that has no name." He grunted and chewed.

"What river? Where is it?"

"Jesus!" he shouted. "You men wanna be paid?" The captain shook his head, sending his black hair flying. "All I can tell you. I found it by accident one day when my navigator took a wrong turn from the Williamette. Good luck." He walked off for closer supervision.

Spur shrugged. A river with no name. One that fed the Williamette. It was a start. He rode to the public library and got a map of the outlying area.

It showed dozens of streams and rivers, most of which emptied into the great body of water that had made the city of Portland what it was.

All of them were named. He put down the map and sighed. How many more were there running through the wilderness? And where was the one that he needed?

He ate, slept soundly that night and rose with the sun. This time he'd ride east and hope he got lucky.

Two hours later, Spur stopped in a shaded glen splashed with the blooms of rhododendrons and Scotch broom. His mare had let him know that she was thirsty. He dismounted, patted its mane and looked around on foot.

Tough, rugged country lay up ahead. The trees seem to bunch together in the distance, just before the land rose up to form a mountain. Its crest was hidden among the pine trees.

No sound of water nearby. No signs of a permanent, wide stream. Nothing.

Damn!

Clare Maxwell's fears materialized as soon as she left DuLac's studio the next day and looked at the twenty dollar-bill in full sunlight. It didn't seem right. She hurried to her hotel room, fuming. Once safely there, the woman retrieved the two fake bills she'd lifted from women and compared them.

They were identical. The money the artist had just given her for her second posing session was counterfeit!

So much for an easy way to earn a living, Clare bitterly thought. She tucked the three bills under her stiff black dress and briefly considered resuming her career as a petty, elderly thief.

Then the face of the artist's girlfriend rose in her mind. She shook it away. No. Too risky. If an able-bodied citizen, or worse, a policeman, happened by and heard a woman screaming that her purse had been stolen by an old lady, they'd stop her, even if they believed that she was aged.

There were always saloons and bawdy houses, but that idea didn't settle well with her. It was too involving, too messy, too disgusting. All those greasy, ill-smelling men pawing her and spreading her legs. She shivered at the picture she'd conjured up.

No. Clare Maxwell sat on her bed and cleared her mind. The best thing to do would be to go back to the artist's studio for one more session. If he gave her another counterfeit bill she'd have to decide what to do.

Emily Curtis peered out of her studio window. After all, she'd promised the fine-looking young man that she'd keep an eye on her fellow artists. Though she was one herself, Emily had never trusted her own kind. The foreign ones were the worst, she thought, nodding as a man dressed in black walked up to Alain DuLac's studio. He went inside.

Nothing unusual about that, unless he was selling one of his paintings. That would be the day!

The white-haired woman checked the clock. An hour until her next appointment. Unless she had unexpected visitors, she had time to think and to remember. Emily Curtis locked the front door and put her hands on her hips. Who should it be today?

Ah, yes—Charles and Mark, her midnight visitors. The young brothers with their barrel chests and furry legs. The men with absolutely identical genitalia that she'd delighted in capturing on canvas.

Where was it? Emily searched for the nude painting, shuffling through the stacks of unfinished pictures that leaned against every available inch of space.

As she looked something stuck in her mind. Alain DuLac, and all those European artists, how did they survive? They might sell one painting every two or three months, but they were always there, working away, using their brushes to scratch together their pitiful ideas of art.

Family money, maybe? She shook her head. Only the most dedicated—or the least talented—stayed on in the artists' colony. But they didn't have an ounce of talent among them. How did an artist like DuLac make a living?

Emily finally found the painting she was looking for. As always, her abilities surprised even her. She gasped as she set the stretched canvas on the easel and settled into the chair she conveniently left in front of it.

The aged artist stared at the image she'd captured on canvas. She constantly scrutinized her work which was why she was so good.

But how does DuLac make his living?

Spur stopped at another stream, far too small to be used for transporting timber. He slid from his rented saddle, stooped and tasted the water. The last rivulet he'd tried was bitter with the tannic acid which the slow-moving water had leached from countless leaves.

His horse whickered as he cupped his hands and drank deeply, enjoying its wet coolness. "What is it, girl?" Spur asked, wiping his mouth on his sleeve. "You smell something? Huh?"

Then he did, too. Smoke. Somewhere nearby.

Wary, he tied the horse to a sturdy sapling and ventured into the brush. Stiff branches tugged at his pant legs. It was slow-going, this plowing through centuries of unchecked plant growth.

The woodsy scent grew stronger. Eventually, he saw a pool of bluish smoke gathering in the air several hundred yards away. He steadily approached it.

Spur moved more slowly, silently, like an Indian. He didn't know who had lit the campfire and he sure as hell didn't want to reveal himself too soon. Not before he had the chance to check everything out.

As he gained on the unseen campfire, Spur heard a faint hum in the distance. It grew less faint, rising until he'd identified it. A river. A big, sprawling river from the sound of it. Thousands of gallons of water boiling over half-submerged rocks.

The river with no name?

He gathered up more landmarks to ensure that he could find his horse again and pushed on. The river must lay directly ahead of him, somewhere behind the campfire.

Movement in the brush beside him startled Spur. He froze, waiting, holding his breath as he reached for his colt .45. A squirrel popped into view from behind a rhododendron, jumped onto a bent pine tree trunk and scampered up it, its claws providing a steady grip.

He moved slowly and as silently as possible, his boots making no more sound than a leaf would as it fell from an overhanging branch. A fallen tree trunk, its furrowed bark covered with moss and iridescent mushrooms, lay across the underbrush. As he stepped over it, Spur's boot broke one of the fantastic looking growths sending white seeds spurting into the air.

The smoke was much stronger now. It started filtering into the air overhead him. He heard a man whistling and the sound of him breaking sticks into firewood.

Spur rounded an ancient oak tree. A brown creature reared up on its hind legs and bellowed at him, paws flashing through the air, saliva drooling from its lower lip.

The bear crashed toward him.

CHAPTER SEVEN

Spur's right hand slashed down to his holster as he sidestepped the advancing brown bear. The animal roared in fury. A paw went up and knocked the Colt .45 from McCoy's grip, sending it hurtling through the air.

Hell!

Unarmed, he was no match for 200 pounds of hairy, enraged power. He dove for his weapon and searched the thick layer of leaves. The bear landed on all fours behind him. Spur felt sudden, intense pressure on his left pant leg and heard the claws tearing and shredding the stiff blue material, dragging him backward.

Shit!

He locked his hands around a thin tree trunk and pulled, forcing his body along the ground away from danger. The pressure on his pants leg released.

Spur instantly stood and shot a look behind him.

The bear panted, staring balefully up at him, sniffing the air. It sat back and raised its huge, wet nose, inhaling a new strange odor.

Food. Frying bacon.

Spur remembered the campfire he'd smelled. He glanced down at the leaves and spied the butt of his Colt.

The bear silently wandered off toward the evocative scent.

Relieved, he retrieved his weapon. A split second after it was firmly in hand, a deep howl of terror ripped through the quiet forest.

Damnit, McCoy thought. He crashed through the underbrush toward the sound.

The trees gave way. He saw a thin man backing from the bear as it poked at the pan set over a small, smoky fire.

"What—what—" he said, looking at Spur.

"Don't move. It doesn't want us anymore—just that." He motioned toward the pan with his revolver.

"Yeah. I guess!"

"Let's just wait!"

The curious bear's nostrils flared. Globules of fat exploded from the strips of meat frying in the pan. The beast pawed it, spilling the cast iron utensil from its perch on the fire. The flames, fed by the bacon grease, roared up as the bear thrust its paw into the fire.

It bellowed in agony, stood and lumbered toward the cringing man.

Spur fired, sending a slug through the animal's heart. It danced on its thick hind legs, turned around, pathetically grunted and slumped onto the fire. Its bulky form quickly smothered the flames.

"Jesus Christ! Is it dead?" the skinny man asked.

"Yeah. I'd figure as much. In any case, it's no threat to us." He slid his revolver into the holster strapped onto his right leg.

The fair-haired man pulled off his hat and slicked the sweat from his forehead. "I don't know what to say. I mean, Jesus! I left my rifle on my mount."

"Not a smart thing to do in this country."

"Yeah."

He was a young man, about 25, but his face was lined and burned by the wind and sun. An outdoors man.

"You should be more careful."

"You sound like my father. I don't know, I just wanted to get away for a while." He shook his head. "So. Who do I have to thank for saving my life?"

"Spur McCoy."

"I'm Jason Miller."

They briefly shook hands over the bear's body.

"I'd heard those things were around here," Jason said, staring down at it. "Never seen one afore."

"You have now."

"Look," Jason said, shaking his head. "Least I can do is get you a cup of coffee."

"Not on that fire you can't."

He smiled. "Right. You got a horse?"

Spur nodded.

"Then come on back to my place. I'll get you the best cup of coffee this side of the Mississippi."

"Is it far?"

"Nope." He shook his head.

"Wait a minute, I'll be right back."

McCoy quickly found his horse and led it through the difficult area. By the time he'd returned, Jason

Miller was mounted and ready to go.

"Come on. It's just a few miles."

They were off, riding through the fir forest. As he bucked in his saddle Spur wondered who the man was and what he was doing out there.

"You got a cabin nearby or something?" Spur yelled as eight hooves crashed through the small bushes and mounds of brown pine needles.

"Or something. You'll see soon enough."

Interesting. Spur realized they were following a rude, seldom-used trail. The smaller trees had been cut off at the ground and, at some time in the past, the bushes cleared away to allow for easier passage.

No single man living in the wilderness would go to that much trouble, Spur thought.

Ahead, through the towering firs, he saw glints of molten silver. Then he heard it again, the sound that had run through the background during his encounter with the brown bear.

They crashed through the trees onto a rocky ridge. Twenty feet below, a huge, flat river flowed along, snaking through the canyon it had carved.

Things were looking up, Spur thought. He smiled. "I don't know the local terrain," he said as Jason smiled over at him. "What river's that?"

"Who the hell knows? We call it the Miller River. Almost there. Come on!"

Jason's horse surged forward as he kicked its flanks. Spur pushed his mare to its limits and caught up with the young man.

The ridge gently lowered, nearing the level of the river. They rounded a bend and, just past the trees, Spur saw it.

Buildings dotted a natural valley right on the edge of the water. A rude dock extended into the deep, blue river. Several men moved around, working at various tasks. Lumber was piled up on the dock. Huge trees, stripped of their branches, lay in stacks beside the river.

A logging camp. A sawmill. It had to be!

Spur smiled as they rode into the camp and halted before a large, well-built house. They tied up their mounts and quickly brushed them down.

"I never would have guessed it," Spur said. "A big operation like this in the middle of nowhere."

Jason shrugged. "It's no problem with the river." He looked at the horses and threw down his brush. "I guess they'll live. Let's get some grub. My stomach feels like it's splitting in two."

"I know the feeling."

As they went to the door, a dark-skinned man straggled by. In spite of the chilly air his only garment was a pair of ragged jeans that hung halfway down his hips. Bizarre, geometric squares of black ink covered one side of his face. The worker paused, gave Spur a dead-eyed stare and wandered off.

They entered a huge kitchen. Three stoves sat side by side and a larder covered one whole wall. Chickens and rabbits hung by their feet from the ceiling. Piles of freshly-caught fish rested in baskets on a table beside a large collection of gleaming knives.

A huge pot bubbled on one of the stoves, sending the warming, stomach-churning scent of food through the air.

"Yep. Should be ready. Cookie always keeps something on the stove in case one of us gets the hungries," Jason said, pulling two huge pewter bowls and spoons from a cupboard.

He ladled the thick, beef-rich stew into the bowls and slapped them down on the table.

"Have a seat and stuff your face," Jason said with glee. "Hell, this meal's on me."

As he ate, Spur held back his questions. No reason to seem too interested just yet. He'd bide his time.

Emily Curtis shook her head. That man had been in Alain DuLac's studio for far too long. Besides, the elderly woman thought as she pushed her rocking chair toward the window, he was no art lover. No art lover would go near that man's place.

She sighed and settled into the quilt-strewn chair. Though she didn't spend all her time spying on her neighbors, she did like to keep up with the art colony's doings. Emily shook her head.

As a matter of fact, a lot of strange men had gone into DuLac's place lately. She'd noticed because she thought maybe he'd become popular or some other nonsense. But the woman couldn't remember seeing some of them come back out again.

Emily Curtis, she told herself, mind your own business. You've that Carter girl's portrait to finish by five o'clock. You have little time for this foolishness, she scolded herself.

She rose and felt the old pain flare up in her knees again. That handsome man she'd talked to would just have to find someone else to tell him the local gossip.

"How long has this place been running?" Spur asked before biting into a crusty slice of bread.

"Little over a year." Jason burped and pushed away his empty bowl.

"Doing well?"

"Yeah, I'd say we're doing fine. Lots of orders, lots of sales, little overhead."

"Some kind of foreigners working for you, right?" Spur washed down the bread with a sip of whiskey.

"Yep. They work for a lot less than men from around here would. That helps us cut our costs and lowers our prices. It's good business."

Though the man's words were calm and rational, Spur noticed Jason tightening his lips. A vein throbbed in the young man's neck. What was going on here?

He decided to throw out the bait. "You wouldn't be interested in an outside investor, would you?"

Miller smiled. "Shore! I'd have to talk to the old man about it, but it's nothing he hasn't said before." He wiped a brown splotch from his chin and gave a satisfying, open-mouthed burp. "I'll see if I can find him. Just help yourself to anything else if you're not full. Be right back."

Jason Miller disappeared through a door.

Well, McCoy thought as he spooned the last of the stew into his mouth, things were moving along better than he'd thought they would. He'd found the camp. The solitary worker he'd seen so far—the one with all those stains all over his face—sure wasn't an Indian. A Hawaiian?

Probably.

He took another shot of whiskey, remembering a book General Halleck had in his library back home. The leather-bound volume was the record of some sea captain's voyage to the Sandwich Islands, or Hawaii, as it was starting to be called.

If Jason Miller and his father were running a slavery operation here, it was time they were stopped. He set his muslin napkin on the table and rubbed his gut. He'd have to learn as much about the place as he could before shutting it down. So he'd stay put for a while, gathering as much information as he could.

The outer door banged open.

"What in tarnation—"

Spur just had time to duck under the table as a weapon spoke, peppering the kitchen walls with shot.

CHAPTER EIGHT

The explosions echoed through the logging camp kitchen. The unseen man's yells were just audible above the blasts that ricocheted around the large room.

Crouching under the plank table, Spur figured he wasn't in any real danger, but he drew just in case. He heard the sounds of the man re-loading his shotgun.

"What in Sam Hell's going on here?" the man demanded in an authoritative voice.

"Calm down!" Spur shouted.

"Calm down? Christ, I find a stranger sitting at my own goddamn table!"

"Jason Miller brought me her," Spur yelled.

"Bull!" he snorted.

"Ask him!"

"You gotta do better than that. My son'd never do something that dumbass. Stand up so I can kill you properly!"

"Your son just went looking for you," Spur told the elder Miller. He sighed and rose to his feet, armed and ready for a fight. "Talk to him before you go killing me!"

Miller sweetened his aim. "I don't gotta talk to him to know trouble!" The oily man grinned.

Spur threw his revolver onto the table. "Didn't your mother ever teach you any table manners?"

"No," a voice said from behind Spur. "And he didn't teach me none neither!"

The elder Miller slightly lowered his aim. "Jason! What the hell is this man doing here?"

"Put that thing away!" Jason strode up to Spur and laid his arm around McCoy's shoulder. "Unless you want to kill the man who just saved my life!"

"Don't talk to me like that, boy!" The short haired, beady eyed man advanced on the pair. "You expect me to believe that crap?"

Spur felt Jason tense beside him. "Drop your weapon or I walk outa here right now, old man! I mean it!"

Miller frowned. "You wouldn't!"

"Try me!"

He sputtered, grumbled and laid the shotgun on the table.

"That's better, pop!"

Spur shrugged off Jason's arm. "You got one hell of a way of greeting your guests, Miller."

"Is that true? What he just said?"

"Yeah. If I hadn't run into your son out in the woods some bear'd be burping him up right now." Spur shook his head. "You can thank me later— when you relax."

The middle-aged man scowled, deepening the creases in his crimson face. "How can I relax? Hell,

I got labor problems. Some of my men aren't working their fair share."

"Can you blame them?"

Miller shot his son a piercing glance.

Spur looked between the two men. "Thanks for the grub, Jason. See you later."

"No. Wait, McCoy!" Jason turned to his father. "You know how you're always talking about bringing in some new money? Getting a partner to expand our operation out here in this hell-hole?"

"Yeah." Miller's eyes were guarded. He switched his gaze from Spur to his son. "Go on."

"The man you almost killed—the one who saved my life—just might be interested."

Harry Miller raised his eyebrows and tried to smile. His face was so tight that he couldn't manage more than a lopsided grin. "Ah, well, hell! Can't blame a guy for tryin' to protect his business. No hard feelin's, right, McCoy?"

"Right." Spur nodded.

"How much would you be willing to invest?" Harry walked to a small table and poured himself a glass of whiskey.

"I don't know. I'd have to look around the place first. See what kind of operation you're running."

"About that—" Jason began.

"What my boy's trying to say is that this isn't your ordinary logging camp."

"I figured as much. Heard some tales about this place—nothing definite, just that you sell lumber cheaper than anyone in town. A real good buy."

Harry Miller stared at him. "So?"

Spur smiled. "So I'm interested. I don't care how you cut your costs, Miller. All I'm concerned about is getting my money's worth."

"Dad, we could get a new mill. Double our output of lumber in a few months!"

"Yeah. Yeah." He bolted down the whiskey and poured another drink.

"Hey, Miller, I'm not squeamish. You do what you gotta do to make a dollar. Right?"

He was silent.

"So I don't care about that." Spur spoke slowly. "I don't care about anything but money. Understand?"

Miller brightened. "Yeah. Yeah sure!"

Spur smiled. Time to draw them in. "Okay. Just to give you two something to chew over, how's, oh, $10,000 sound?"

The man spit up the liquor.

"Ten thousand?" Jason grinned at him. "That sounds fine to me. More than fine! How about it, old man?"

Harry Miller sat at the table and nodded. "Sounds good. I import the finest labor money can buy. Bring those god-forsaken pagans all the way across the ocean. Give them naked savages jobs, a place to bunk and something to eat."

"Barely," Jason threw in.

Spur watched the two men lock gazes, realizing just how deep the conflict ran between them.

"It sounds good to me." Miller peered up at Spur. "As long as you understand you're just a money man. Don't go trying to change the way I run things around here."

"You're getting ahead of yourself. I haven't said I'll invest yet," Spur pointed out. "I need to study your figures, look at the future of your operation, see if it's worth my while."

"Yeah. Yeah! You can stay here for a few days.

Isn't that right, father?"

"Of course. Hell, be glad to have you around."

Jason went to the elder Miller. "Just think of it! We could set up the new mill and hire more help. Maybe treat 'em better, not work 'em so hard, so they won't di—ah, I mean, quit on us so fast." He faintly smiled at Spur.

"Yeah. Okay. You look over the place, McCoy. Take Jason with you and ask him questions. I'd do it myself but I'm too busy. Always too damned busy." He coughed.

"Fine. I'll let you know before I leave."

Harry Miller rose and looked at his son. "Git your ass outa here!" he bellowed.

"Right, old man."

"And don't call me that!"

"You promised me this wouldn't happen again!" Rebecca Ledet said, pouting and crossing her arms.

"I—I could not help it."

"Sure." She rolled her eyes.

"Your friends—"

"It wouldn't do any good." The girl frowned.

"Why not? They helped you before?" Alain felt an unusual sensation flooding through his body. It was tight, harsh and made him queasy.

"They just won't take your money any more, Alain. I warned you but you wouldn't listen. It's time you dumped that printing press in the river and concentrate on your painting, on earning an honest living!"

"You sound like my dead wife." Alain rubbed his chest.

"How could you compare me to that ugly troll?" Rebecca held her chin high.

He winced. "In the meantime, what do we do with him?" He pointed to the lifeless form lying in the center of his studio, slowly oozing life onto the floor.

"He doesn't look very big," Rebecca said. "Can't you handle it yourself?"

"Myself. Myself!" Alain knocked over his easel. "Myself? Why do you think I have kept you around?"

Rebecca sucked in her breath and shook her head.

"I—I mean—"

She shrank away from him, backing toward the wall.

"You *bastard!* I thought you loved me!"

"I love your face, your body!" DuLac shook his head. "I cannot love a woman. Any woman! My wife destroyed that in me. I told you that!"

"You just keep me around to get to my friends. Right?" The hardened girl laughed. "You never cared about me. Ever!" She stormed off to the bedroom, her skirts swirling behind her.

"What are you doing?" Alain asked, stepping over the dead man's body.

Silks and crinolines flew from the closet onto the bed. "Packing. I'm going to Madame Burchard's. She said I could stay at her house any time I wanted."

"Rebecca. Please! The body!"

The beautiful girl spun toward him. "That's all you care about. Bodies! Well this body's leaving. I don't care what you do with the other one!"

"No. No!"

"Don't worry, Alain. I won't tell a soul what kind of man you are. Not a word! But if you ever try to touch me again, I'll—I'll—" Rebecca shook her head and stuffed her belongings into the leather bags.

"I bought you all those things!" Alain walked into the bedroom.

"Sure. And I earned them—on my back!"

She flipped the cases closed and pushed past him. "Really, Alain," Rebecca said as she unlocked the front door, "If you didn't kill every man who walked in here, we might still be together."

He locked the door as soon as she'd bounded outside and turned toward the dead man. What, oh what was he going to do?

"You don't seem to get along with your father," Spur said as he walked with Jason Miller.

The man's thin features darkened. "That's no secret. He's changed. As soon as he got the idea of starting this business, sold the house in Portland and set up camp here, something seemed to snap inside him. The way he treats those men—" He sighed. "That's why we need you, McCoy. Your money could turn this into a normal, legal operation." Jason stopped. "You don't know how many men have died."

"Accidents?"

"I wish! Overwork, mostly. The old man seems

to think that a bowl of soup and a cup of water every day is enough for the Hawaiians. Not when they're working from sunup to sundown."

"He really is a bastard, isn't he?"

"Yeah." Jason Miller scratched his side. "But you can change all that, McCoy. I hate what he's done here, what he's done to the men."

"Can't you do anything? Can't you talk some sense into the man?"

"No. Only other thing I could do is walk out of here. But he's got me so involved I can't leave. Besides, if I turned him in he'd accuse me of cooking up the whole scheme. I'd wind up on the end of a rope right alongside that bastard—if he didn't kill me first."

Spur was silent.

Jason sighed. "That's the mill over there, obviously. We use a vertical saw. Right now we've got fifty men working for us. Most of them are out cutting down trees. We go into places that aren't easily visible, that wouldn't attract attention. We float half the logs for sale to a landing downstream, but not all the way to the Williamette. The rest we cut right here, haul them down to our outpost and load them onto our customers' ships. That's only after we've got the cash in hand. We cut to order, whatever they want."

"I see."

Jason's voice was dull, even-toned. "My father sails into town once a week, taking orders. Everything's done on the sly, mostly at night. Our lumber goes all over the place." He turned to Spur. "Sometimes I wake up at night and hear the men screaming." He shivered.

Spur slapped Jason's shoulder. "I gotta feeling

all that's gonna change. Mighty soon."

Jason looked at him and smacked his lips. "So what are you saying? You'll invest?"

McCoy nodded. "Yeah. I'll invest."

CHAPTER NINE

As Spur walked around the logging operations, he flinched at the looks of outright hatred the indentured workers flashed at him whenever he came upon them. Jason Miller hadn't been exaggerating when he described his father's treatment of the men. Things were ripe for a revolution.

Male shouts issued from the saw mill. Jason grimaced and slapped Spur's shoulder.

"I'll go see what the trouble is," he said and ran off to the sturdily-built structure.

Spur walked behind the mill, unwilling to get involved in the matter, and studied the river with no name. It was broad, deep and flat. He could tell it was deep from the hue of the water that swiftly flowed through its center. A solitary boat bobbed at the dock.

They must have other boats out. He was surprised by the lack of horses but then again, too many of them around might tempt the workers.

McCoy frowned and stared at the water. The sound of boots rapidly approaching him made Spur look up. An elderly, haggard-faced man rushed up.

"Who the hell are you?" he asked, holding a small black bag.

McCoy raised his hands. "Don't start shooting. I'm with Jason Miller."

The white-hair harumphed. "Some damn fool musta got himself all cut up in there." Doc hurried by and disappeared into the saw mill.

A stiff wind swept through the clearing, sending the towering pines whispering far above where nature took over from the works of men. Spur pulled his coat more tightly around him. The chill in the air surprised him. It didn't snow in spring up here in Oregon, did it?

As Spur was wondereing about it, a brown-skinned man stumbled out from the mill. His face was nearly blocked by the huge armload of firewood that had been piled onto him.

The slave, the human merchandise that Harry Miller had purchased from overseas, shivered as the wind cut through the torn jeans that were his only clothing. Moving shakily across the uneven ground, the man's bare foot crashed down on a sharp rock.

The firewood spilled to the ground, revealing the tattoo-covered face of the worker he'd seen earlier.

"Damnit!"

The curse was heavily accented. The Hawaiian threw up his hands and stared down at the wood.

It was a good time to make a move, Spur thought

as he walked up to him. "Let me help you."

The slave turned violently toward him and shook his head.

"Come on! How often do you get a white man saying that to you?"

Nearing the slave, Spur was shocked at his appearance. He was pathetically thin. The ribs were clearly visible under his skin. How old was he? Eighteen? Nineteen?

He proudly shook his head again, shivering.

"Look, son. There's no way you can pile all that wood onto your arms without some help." Spur squatted and picked up four heavy, thick pieces of oak firewood. "Are you gonna cooperate with me?"

Silence. A tight-lipped, angry stare.

"What's your name?"

"What is yours?"

At least he hadn't had his tongue cut out. "Spur McCoy."

He looked down at the ground. "I'm Kimo. Here they call me Mike."

"Well, Kimo, will you take this or are you going to let me stand here and look like a fool?"

He lowered his eyes and grabbed the wood. "Thanks."

Another Hawaiian man rushed from the sawmill toward the main house. He stared curiously at Spur and Kimo as he passed.

"How'd you like to get out of here? Go back home?" Spur asked.

Kimo grunted. "Yes."

Spur smiled. "I thought so."

The front door of the main house banged open. Spur turned to see Harry Miller, his face blood-red, charging toward the sawmill.

Kimo flinched at the sight of his boss.

Do something, Spur told himself. "And don't let me catch you dropping this shit all over the place again!" he yelled in a voice loud enough for Harry to hear.

The man barely acknowledged McCoy's presence as he rushed to where he had been summoned.

Kimo looked up at the white man with blank eyes. He shrugged.

Spur laid his hand on the man's shoulder. Kimo's skin, used to the balmy sun of the tropics, was icy. "Look. I can help you get home."

"No. No one can help."

"*I* can. But I need you with me."

"I already have a death sentence. I don't want to hurry that." Kimo stooped to retrieve another piece of wood.

Spur took it out of his hands. He looked around and saw the stables. "Come on. Let's get rid of this firewood."

Between the two of them they carried it to the woodshed outside of the house. Kimo started to walk away but Spur grabbed his shoulder and ushered him into the stables.

A very pregnant mare regarded them with huge brown eyes as he led the slave into the relative warmth and comfort of the stinking building.

Spur sloughed off his jacket and held it out. When Kimo regarded it with suspicious eyes, Spur cursed and slipped it around the man's shoulders.

"Why are you doing this?" Kimo demanded in far too loud a voice. "You are a white men like all the others!"

"No. I'm not! Listen to me, Kimo. The government is very interested in Harry Miller. I'm here to shut him down, to take him to jail."

Kimo raised his eyebrows, animating the checkered pattern that extended from his left jawbone to his hairline. "And then I could return home?"

"Yes. Yes, of course!"

He stuffed his arms into the jacket and held it around his still shivering body. "Oh."

"What's been happening here?"

"Three of my friends are gone."

Spur shook his head. "Gone?"

"Died. My brother is dead. Fell a long way when topping a tree—that's what they said."

"How did you get here?"

Kimo sighed. "A white man came to Maui and said he was hiring strong men to work on the Mainland. I signed up with many of my friends. When we got here, they treated us like animals." He glanced at the mare. "Worse than that. Work all day. Chains at night." Kimo sat on the ground and rubbed his feet against the straw-covered dirt, allowing himself the luxury of trying to get warm. "They said I could send for my wife later. I can't," he spat, staring at the ground. "No women allowed. And I have not seen my baby since it was born."

Spur shook his head. "Then I can count on you for help? At any time?"

Kimo nodded. "Yes. Any time."

The mare whinneyed. She was going into labor.

"You'd, ah, better get back to work."

Kimo reluctantly stood, slipped the jacket from his shoulders and gave it back to his benefactor as he walked out of the stable. The man returning to work seemed to hold his shoulders a bit higher, Spur thought.

Spur blew onto his hands and went outside. That night he'd find out what sort of security arrangements Harry had. He assumed they'd be heavy.

Three hours later, he was again talking with Jason Miller. He'd found out much of what he wanted to know. The men were indeed kept in ankle chains at night as they slept in the huge, long barracks that were set up in the middle of the clearing. Four armed guards were stationed on each side of the rectangular building and two inside it. A pair of additional guards roamed the perimeter of the area through the trees on horseback, just in case any of the men managed to escape.

Eight men plus Harry Miller. How could he break the news to Jason, Spur wondered, looking at the young man.

Jason halted his endless conversation. "You got something on your mind, McCoy?"

"Ah, no. Just thinking about your workers."

"If you join us we can do something about them."

"I can't believe your father thought he could get away with this!"

Jason shook his head. "The old man moved into Alabama about ten years before the war. I grew up on a plantation surrounded by slaves. He lost everything, including his wife, during the war. As far as he's concerned, the Emancipation Proclamation only related to Africans. I don't think he believes the Hawaiians are human."

Spur stared at Jason.

A bell rang nearby. "Time for grub," Miller said.

That night Spur lay wide awake, fully dressed, in the simply furnished room. He peered out the window at the barracks where the fifty men were kept. The only guard he could see stood there, rifle slung over his shoulder, constantly vigilant. His back was toward Spur and remained that way for as long as he looked. The man wasn't concerned about anyone breaking in—just getting out.

During a short, post-food conference in Harry Miller's panelled office, one of the guards had walked in and handed Harry a large key ring. "They're locked up," the grizzled man had said as Miller stashed the keys in his drawer.

Another piece of the puzzle. Spur realized he could ride back into town in the morning, get as much help as Commissioner Golden could spare and charge up there, eventually freeing the men. But the cost in lives on both sides would be heavy. Too heavy.

No. He had to do something tonight. Now.

Spur remained in his room until the house had been quiet for hours. Alert, ready for action, he worked out his plan, trying to account for every contingency, drawing up alternatives to keep in reserve.

He walked to the small clock, wincing as the floorboards groaned under his weight. The thin black hands revealed the hour: 2.13. It was time.

Another quick look out the window showed the thin moon starting its slide down the western sky. Nothing had changed—the guards were all in place.

Spur slipped out of his room and silently padded down the stairs. He turned left at the landing, thankful for the thick carpets that cushioned his boots, and made his way to Harry Miller's office.

The door was ajar but the room was dark. He walked into the man's office. Thin light issuing from the four lowered flames allowed him to move around without bumping into things.

Spur went to the desk and tried the drawer. It opened, much to his surprise. Harry Miller must not worry about things like locks. After all, he kept his enemies shackled at night.

He reached inside the drawer. Dried pens, bottles of ink, envelopes and other business supplies passed under his hand. Spur quietly, quickly searched for his prize.

A soft clink halted his fingers. He grasped the cold iron ring and smiled. Spur stuffed the keys into his coat pocket and walked toward the door. Just as he touched it a dark figure burst inside, nearly knocking him over.

"What the hell are you doing here?" Harry Miller demanded, turning up the kerosene lamp and staring him down.

CHAPTER TEN

"Well?" Miller yelled, blocking the entrance to his office. "What the hell are you doing here?"

Spur straightened his back and stared directly into the man's eyes, challenging him. "I had some things to talk over with you. Figured you might still be up. That's all, Miller!"

"Yeah, well," the oily man said, frowning. "I'm here. Now, anyway."

"Look, Miller, don't be so damn suspicious of everything and everyone!"

He laughed. "That's my business, McCoy. To be suspicious. I can't help it."

"If you ran your business differently, you wouldn't have that problem."

Harry grunted and moved to his desk. "How true, how true. McCoy, no one's forcing you to buy into this dump," he said as he sat. "Hell, if I paid my

workers anything like real wages, or got regular
hire ons, I wouldn't clear enough money to make
the whole damn thing worthwhile. You're a
businessman; you know that."

"Lots of others get by."

"Yeah, well, I'm tired of getting by."

"What are you working toward?" Spur fell into
a chair facing the man's desk. "You must be making
plenty of money but I certainly don't see it around
here."

Harry Miller smiled. "I'm salting it away in
various banks in town. Keeping it for a rainy day."

Spur thought about the keys in his pocket. "So
you'll eventually get out of here? Close the business,
move into Portland and have a regular life?"

Miller shrugged. "Something like that, but I don't
have to tell you—" He stopped and lightened his
voice. "Sorry. Short-fused, that's me." He scratched
his head. "I haven't decided yet, but I'm working
for the future."

"The here and now seems more important to me."

Harry Miller frowned and reached for his desk
drawer. "That's because you're young."

"Not much younger than you are," he pointed out.

"Your outlook sure as hell is." Miller pulled on
the drawer.

High-pitched screams pierced the night. The man
winced at the sound. "Damn. I'm going back to
bed," he said, slamming the drawer shut.

"Aren't you going to find out what's going on?
Sounds bad to me."

"You'll get used to that, McCoy." He smiled. "One
of the boys acting up again, most likely. Happens
all the time." He rose and left Spur sitting in the
chair.

Seconds later he was out of the house and walking swiftly toward the barracks. The guard at the main door stiffened as he tapped on his shoulder.

"I'm going in," McCoy said, shouting above the screams that issued from the building.

The guard shrugged beneath his dirty hat and spat. "Saw you with Miller before. Okay."

Spur opened the door and walked inside.

Twenty lanterns blazed along the walls, lighting up the place as if it were day. It smelled of dirty clothes, filthy bedding and unwashed human bodies.

Thin cotton blankets lay on either side of a central aisle. Each one held a man. Rows of iron chains extended from one worker to another, fastened to the worker's ankles, binding them to their inhuman life at the mill. Most of the exhausted Hawaiians were sitting up on the miserable beds, staring in mute, accustomed horror at the sight.

One guard held down a young Hawaiian. Another stood over him. The thick leather strap cut into the man's bare back, bubbling it with welts. Each stroke sent him writhing and coiling on the bare, cold floor.

Another vicious slap of leather against skin brought blood seeping from the man's back.

"Don't you talk back to me, boy!" the man said as he whipped him. "Keep your mouth shut!"

"Beat him good, Felton!" the second guard said, grinning as he secured the man's arms.

The skin turned to bright red ribbons of torn flesh. The man blubbered and fell silent, his voice exhausted, his spirit broken by the brutal whipping.

"What is going on here?" Spur yelled, storming

up to the pair.

The shackled Hawaiians lining the walls stared at Spur in stunned silence. Felton let his raised belt hang in the air, dropping his jaw in surprise.

"Who the hell are you?" he demanded.

"Spur McCoy, part-owner of this business—your new boss."

Felton glanced uncertainly at the second white man. "That true, Davis?"

"Yeah, yeah. Heard Jason and the old man chewing it over today."

"Well, so?" Felton demanded.

"Sorry to interrupt your fun, but that stops. Now!" He grabbed the belt and wrestled it from the man's hand. "No more beatings!"

"Hey!"

"Don't talk back to me!" Spur warned him, shaking the belt. "You do and I'll see Miller takes care of you just like he takes care of these men!"

Felton stepped backward. "Hell, no one told me anything's changed. It ain't my fault!"

Spur looked down at the bleeding man, who'd slumped into unconsciousness. "You've been told!"

"Well, well, shit!"

"Come on, Felton," Davis said, rising from his squat. "Let's play cards."

The two men wandered over to a table and chairs strategically stationed beside a small wood-burning stove that let out just enough heat to warm them but kept the rest of the building chilly. They turned their backs on Spur and slapped the devil's pasteboards onto the table.

A hundred eyes stared at McCoy. Spur searched them until he found a familiar face. He looked hard at the man and smiled.

Kimo nodded.

"Davis, get the doc here. That man need medical attention or he'll die before morning."

"He'll die anyway."

Spur stormed to the man. He hauled up the chair and dumped Davis to the ground. "Move your butt!"

"Okay, okay!" he said.

"Miller always told us we weren't supposed to leave for nothing," Felton said as the second guard disappeared.

"I'm in charge now." Spur's voice was pointed.

"Well, what the hell." Felton returned to shuffling the cards.

Spur stepped five paces away and looked over his shoulder. The man showed him his back. He held a finger up to his lips, studying the Hawaiians, who nodded at his silent signal.

He drew his Colt and silently moved back to the table. Spur brought the butt end of his weapon down hard on the man's skull. Felton grunted and slumped forward.

The Hawaiians murmured.

One down, one out of the way for the moment, four outside. He threw the keys to Kimo. "Hurry. Get them all unlocked but lay there like you're still shackled. Understand?"

Kimo nodded and plunged the key into the iron bands surrounding his ankles.

"Hey!" Spur yelled toward the door. "I need some help in here!"

"That you, Felton?"

"Just get in here!"

The man appeared. Spur blasted him full of lead.

Kimo, freed, hustled from man to man.

"Two of you men take him to the far corner,"

Spur said, pointing at the wounded slave, "where he won't get trampled. Then lie down like you're still chained."

The pair of newly freed men stared at each other and hauled the man away.

The Hawaiians whispered to each other as Kimo worked on them. He was fast. The two men returned to their pallets and laid the opened shackles around their ankles.

A few more minutes, Spur thought, and every worker would be free.

The elderly doctor walked in, his head toward the floor. "What's so important that I have to get up in the middle of the night?" He saw Felton slumped on the table, then the Hawaiian moving among his own.

"Hey!"

Spur patted him down. The man wore no weapons. "There's a Hawaiian bleeding to death in the corner, doc! If you wanna be breathing in the morning you go save his life. And do it quietly!"

The white-haired doc froze, then nodded. He walked towards the downed man.

Spur took up his position beside the door, his Colt drawn. The wooden rectangle opened and Davis burst inside along with one of the exterior guards.

"Something fishy goin' on—hey!"

"Drop your weapons!" Spur said.

They stared at him. McCoy fired before Davis's finger could pull the trigger. The second guard managed to peel of a wide shot before Spur silenced his revolver and the man himself.

"Hurry, Kimo! The whole place is gonna come crashing down on us in five seconds!"

"Okay, okay!"

Loud voices outside. Shouts. Spur slipped fresh rounds into the empty chambers. He thought he might need them.

Kimo unlocked the last pair of shackles and scurried over to him.

McCoy pocketed the keys and Kimo silently took his position on his pallet. The Hawaiians were excited, their eyes alert at the new feeling that help just might have found them.

"What the hell you talking about, Riley?"

He recognized the voice before Jason Miller walked in.

"Look, Jason," Spur said as the man faced him. "You've got a chance. Help me or you're dead."

"I—I—"

"No time for that!" Spur yelled. "Help me get your father or you'll hang too."

Jason Miller shrugged and drew his weapon. "Okay." He hardened his face.

Spur retrieved the revolvers from the dead guards and a still unconscious Felton. He handed them to Kimo, who quickly distributed the weapons to the men who sat on their side of him.

"Keep those firing irons out of sight. Use them only when I tell you to!"

"Right!'

"Sorry," the doctor said from the far side of the barracks. "He's cut up too badly. Nothing I can do for him."

"Try, goddamnit!" Spur shouted.

He turned toward the door, waiting, itching for the whole thing to start.

The outside guards weren't coming in.

"What the hell's going on in there?" Harry Miller asked.

Jason turned to Spur and nodded.
McCoy sighed. He'd never led a revolution before.

CHAPTER ELEVEN

"Miller, get in here!" Spur shouted out of the barracks.

"That you, McCoy?"

"Yeah, it's me."

"What the hell you think you're doing? Give me some answers, boy!"

"Come in and find out!"

Silence. Spur glanced around the room—at the doctor who looked up from the man who was bleeding to death, at Kimo and his friends who, against his orders, held the unfamiliar weapons he'd given them in shaky hands, at Jason Miller who stood solidly on the bare earthen floor, at the dead guards near his feet.

From the table, Felton grunted and lifted his head. Spur gave him another knock to the skull. He quieted as his chin hit the wooden surface.

"I'm waiting, Miller! Or don't you care what's happening in here?"

"No. You come out here!"

"I hold all the cards. You scared, Miller? Afraid to confront the monster you've created, the monster that's spitting up in your face?"

"Damn you! I got two men with me!"

Spur laughed. "And I've got your son!"

Again, silence. Jason started to speak but Spur held up his hand.

"You holding my boy against his will? By God, I'll kill you for that!"

"It never bothered you to work these men to death, treating them like slaves! Come on in and get him, Miller! Or aren't you man enough?"

Jason smiled.

The Hawaiians rustled. Spur turned and saw Kimo shrug off the hated shackles and stand. One by one the others rose and stretched.

"You got ten seconds, Miller. Get your fat ass in here or you'll be burying your son at dawn!"

Spur motioned with his weapon to the door. Tension flooded the air. Jason bent toward McCoy's ear.

"If you have to kill him, go ahead," he whispered, his thin features set, hard.

Spur nodded. "Your ten seconds are up, Miller!"

McCoy motioned to Kimo, raised his revolver in the air and pantomimed firing it. The Hawaiian shook his head, widened his eyes and nodded. He lifted the bulky Army revolver, tensed and pulled the trigger.

The resulting surge of energy exiting the barrel sent the man to the floor. The explosion echoed throughout the barracks. Miller's shouts outside were lost by the rush of a hundred feet. The gunshot had triggered the Hawaiians into full-scale revolt. Jason and Spur stood back as they poured from the barracks, whooping and yelling.

"Let's go!"

Spur pushed through them with Jason on his heels. Outside, they saw a figure retreating to the stables. Miller, Spur figured.

"Stay here!" Spur said to the Hawaiian men as he raced to the small building.

Jason ran up to him as McCoy saddled up the closest horse.

"No," he said. "Take Frankie. He's the fastest horse we have."

"Thanks." Spur transferred the saddle and cinched it up.

"I can't go with you. I can't do it."

"I understand, Jason. You'll stick around and keep an eye on things here?"

"Sure," he said. "Just go out and get that bastard!"

Spur mounted and rode into the night.

The horse balked at the new rider, fighting Spur, snorting and refusing to respond to his commands. Damnit, he thought, as he coaxed the beast. Come on!

Miller had ridden east, past the main house, into the virgin forest. Spur had no idea of his destination but it was clear that Miller hadn't wanted a confrontation. He couldn't blame the man—152 to 3 odds weren't very heartening.

He'd seen no signs of the two remaining guards. They'd probably fled as well.

The horse finally warmed to him. Spur kicked its flanks and the gelding bolted forward, crashing

through the underbrush, veering to the left and
right of the sturdy trees that rushed up on both
sides.

The moon gave little light and half of that was
blocked out by overhead branches. Spur saw the
signs of the man's passing, though—broken
saplings and trampled bushes. Phosphorescent
fungus hanging from the pine tree limbs and
festooning long-dead trunks lent its own eerie glow
to his passage.

Fast. Faster.

Spur charged through the wilderness. He topped
a small hill and started down the other side. In the
distance he saw the glint of the nameless river
where it bent on its way to the Williamette.

A rider approached him from the rear. Spur
didn't have time to see who it was. Maybe Jason had
changed his mind.

He broke through the trees into a recently cleared
section of land. The tree tops bobbed up and down,
hiding and revealing the crescent moon. He pushed
his mount as hard as he could for as long as he
could.

A copse of trees loomed up ahead. Just before
they enveloped him Spur turned back. From 50 feet
behind him the rider fired a shot.

One of the guards. Must have figured out I wasn't
his employer, Spur thought, and lost himself in the
trees. At the same time, Miller's faint trail vanished.

Spur slowed his horse, dismounted and drew his
revolver. He peeled off a shot as the pursuing guard
crashed by him. The man grunted and disappeared
into the trees. A shoulder hit, McCoy thought,
hurrying back into the saddle.

He held the reins with his left hand, his Colt with

the right, his eyes searching the forest up ahead. This wasn't going well. True, he'd done his job by freeing the men, but if he didn't have Harry Miller locked up or put out of commission, the man'd just do it all over again.

The trees grew thicker, with less space between their trunks. The horse slowed as it sped through the difficult terrain. Spur caught a glimpse of the guard riding hard ahead of him. He gently eased the horse to a faster gallop and carefully fired.

The guard slumped in the saddle. His torso slipped to the right and slammed into a thick tree trunk. The man fell to the ground, broken, dead.

Spur didn't glance down at him as he raced past. Where the hell was Harry Miller?

An hour later, McCoy halted his horse to let it get its breath at a moon-spangled stream. He dismounted and walked the surrounding area. No signs of the man's recent passage. No signs at all.

The forest was holding its secret.

Hell, he thought, staring at the horse's long tongue lapping at the water. What could he do?

Two options. Return to the sawmill and wait for the man's inevitable return to pick up the pieces, or keep heading into the wilderness searching for him.

Miller was smart. He knew the terrain. He wouldn't make a fatal mistake like lighting a fire. He might know of caves where he could hide, tree-shrouded valleys invisible to anyone riding above them. He might even have cabins that dotted the terrain to be used during logging operations.

Spur went to his horse and rubbed its mane, flicking the long, coarse hairs thorugh his fingers.

Then he smiled. What had Jason Miller told him?

They floated the unsawn logs to a second dock down river. Could the man be heading that way?

Harry Miller had been heading south as he rode out of the camp.

It was a chance. Not much of one, but a chance. Adrenaline surged through his veins as Spur mounted up. "Come on!" he urged his horse with his heels.

He angled the horse through the forest, searching for the river, using the moon as his compass. He found it.

An hour later, Spur had followed its meandering course for several miles, looking ahead for his destination. The scene up ahead made him slow his horse.

"There it is," he whispered.

A small building stood on the rock strewn beach. From it, a rude dock extended into the water. A storm must have blown through lately, for the dim moonlight bouncing off the surging water showed jagged, broken planks jutting from the dock's end. The wind-whipped river must have ripped it in half during the storm.

Light glowed in the cabin's window and smoke trailed up from the chimney. Spur walked the horse to within 20 feet of the place and tied it to a tree. He calmed himself and approached the building.

One horse stood at a trough. He cautiously approached it. It started in alarm but Spur grabbed its muzzle and held it, quieting the beast. Sweat foamed on its back. The horse had been ridden hard and brought here only minutes before.

McCoy smiled. He almost had him.

When he'd reassured the horse, he slipped past the window. The curtains were drawn, blocking a clear view, but the shadow of a fire moved between them and the lamp. Spur figured the direct approach would be the best.

He reloaded, moved past the corner of the small house and tried the doorknob. It silently turned— must have been recently oiled. Spur cracked it open an inch. The visible slice of the cabin's interior showed shelves holding dusty cans of food and loaves of bread. Firelight flickered against a wooden chair. Where was the man?

He shook his head and pushed hard on the door. It swung open.

Harry Miller stared down at him from behind his rifle, his finger on the trigger.

"Nice of you to join me, McCoy!"

CHAPTER TWELVE

"I knew you were trouble the first time I laid eyes on you!"

"You never laid anything on me," Spur said to the rifle-toting man.

"Don't get smart with me, McCoy! You thought you could come in and break up my little operation, right? Thought you could ruin my little utopia."

"More like your hell."

"Shut up!" He gestured with his left hand. "Give me your weapon."

Spur grunted. "If you kill me and ride back to your camp, you know what you'll find? Dead guards, at least one dead Hawaiian—and no one else."

"What about my son?"

"You mean Jason? He'd probably meet you with a rifle and splatter your worthless guts all over the trees." He paused. "I wasn't holding Jason against his will. He joined me because he hates the way you've run your camp. He hates you even more and told me to blast you into hell."

Miller laughed. "Nice try, McCoy. My son'd never turn on me."

"He did, because you turned on him. He never expected you to run that place like a pre-war plantation, working the poor bastards to death just to save a few bucks!"

"Shut up!" Miller sweated.

It was working. "You've got blood on your hands, Miller! The blood of innocent men! Oh, you may not have actually killed any of them, but you sentenced them to death in a strange country far from their homes. You're worse than a murderer. You're a slaver."

Miller's face tensed. "Shut the hell up and give me your revolver, goddamnit!"

"Why? So you can kill an unarmed man? So I won't blast a hole through your skull as I drop? No way, Miller! If I'm gonna go, I'll take you with me— to hell!"

Their gazes locked.

"You don't scare too easy," Miller said.

"You've got nothing to go back to."

"The banks! All my money! I don't give a shit about the mill or those damned bastards!"

"Jason'll be in town at dawn and draw out every penny you ever deposited."

"Not if I get their first!"

Hooves pounded outside.

Spur smiled. "That's him now, come to help me kill you, just like we'd planned."

The man faltered. 'No. No!''

Spur fired during the split second that Harry Miller glanced at the door. The big man groaned, blasted the roof and dropped his rifle. His hands went to his chest. Boots rustled outside.

"Harry?" a voice yelled.

"Yeah!" Spur affected the man's throaty voice, moving to the wall near the entrance.

Miller fell to his knees, his face reddening, the veins in his neck popping out. His hands went to his stomach, covering and protecting the wound. "Jesus Christ!"

The door banged open. "Thought you might've—"

Spur rushed the man, easily disarmed him and kicked the rifle across the room.

"You!" the guard said, flustered.

He was young, too young to be involved with the likes of Miller. Sweat gleamed on his youthful features. A moustache was just beginning to sprout on his upper lip.

"Yeah. Me. We're all going back. Give me any trouble, boy, and you'll lose your balls."

Harry Miller bellowed but rose to his feet. "I'll be damned if I'm going anywhere with you!"

"Pipe down." Spur smashed his boot against the man's legs, sending Miller crashing to the floor again. He howled even harder as fiery pain stabbed through him.

"What's your name?" McCoy asked the guard.

"Riley, sir."

"How old are you?"

"Eighteen." He swallowed. "Look, he'll be dead inside an hour. That's a gut-wound. One of the boys at the camp croaked from one of those."

"Who gave it to him?"

Riley nodded toward Miller and frowned.

The boy stiffened under Spur's gaze.

"Hey, look, it was just a job! My dad worked for him and he got me hired on. I didn't know what it was like until I was in up to my ears."

"Right."

"It's true!"

Harry Miller crawled across the floor. Spur watched as the bleeding man's hands clasped the rifle.

"Don't try it!"

"Damn you!"

He levelled the rifle and slammed a shot into the wall. Too close, Spur thought, as he sent another load of hot lead into the man's body. A clean shot. Right through the heart.

Harry Miller would never buy any more slaves.

The big man slumped onto his back, kicked, shuddered and slowly exhaled his way into the next world.

"Wow!" Riley said as he stared at the still man. "He could've killed you!"

"Or you," Spur pointed out.

"Right."

"You gonna cooperate with me?"

"Yessir!" came the ready response.

"Okay. Let's get this man on a horse and head back. Right now, before dawn."

Two hours later, under Riley's guidance, they rode into camp. The boy had fully cooperated with him—out of disgust for his dead boss or because he was out of a job. Either way, Spur was glad he'd happened along.

The place looked deserted, but every light in the two-story house blazed away. Dozens of voices mixed with music issued from the structure. The two men looked at each other as they untied Miller's body and hauled him into the deserted barracks.

"No sense in breaking up the party with this," Spur said.

Riley smiled as they unceremoniously dumped the man onto the cold earth.

The young man sighed, took off his hat and slicked his forehead. "That's a relief."

"Come on."

They walked into the house. Kimo, fully dressed, met them with a revolver. He smiled as he recognized them.

"McCoy!" The Hawaiian glanced at Riley. "What's he doing here? With you?"

"He's okay. Really. Don't worry about him."

Kimo nodded. His tattooed face darkened. "What about Harry Miller?"

"Dead. We just threw his body in the barracks."

A high-pitched giggle sounded above the noise.

Kimo smiled. "We found the things Miller took from us stashed in the house. Kalani even found his ukelele. We are celebrating."

"Great. Is Jason around?"

"Yeah. In there." Kimo raised his eyebrows. "He rode out and brought us some presents that had just arrived. It's not a pretty sight."

Spur looked quizzically at him and shrugged. "You find the other guards?"

"Yes. We killed them."

"Then there's no need for a lookout. Come on, Kimo; show us your party!"

The three men walked into the parlor. Spur wasn't surprised to see dozens of brown-skinned women frolicking with the men. The whole room was a sea of clothed and naked bodies writhing around, locked in the timeless choreography of love. Hips thrust. Mouths locked together. Hands clenched.

The smell of sex-musk hung in the air.

"Wow!" Riley said.

"What's wrong, kid?"

"They even took baths!"

Spur shook his head.

A few of the Hawaiians, already spent, stood back and watched, sucking up the once-forbidden liquor and smoking cigars. One strummed a ukelele and sung in a lyrical, pleasant language.

"McCoy!" a familiar voice called.

Spur laughed as Jason Miller stopped in mid-stroke, pulled out of the blonde woman he'd been lying on top of and walked over to them.

"Can you believe it?" he said, spreading out his hands, taking in the whole room with the gesture.

"Not likely."

Jason smiled. "These girls got suspicious so they took up a collection at their church on Maui. The missionaries even helped them out. Raised enough money to sail over here and get their men back."

Riley loudly swallowed. "They got 'em, alright!"

"I sailed into town to get Commissioner Golden, who told me about the girls. Brought 'em back here two hours after you left." His smile faded. "What about my father?"

"Don't worry about him."

He set his jaw and nodded. "I won't! Have to get

back to business."

Jason dove back into the sea of pumping, sweaty flesh.

A naked woman sprang past them and ran outside, her full breasts bouncing. She laughed as two Hawaiian men chased after her.

Spur turned to Riley. The expression on his face was priceless, he thought, flushed and excited and disbelieving. The sight could be overwhelming.

"Look, son, if you want to leave—" he started.

A bronzed beauty sat in a corner, her face sullen.

"No, that's okay. Excuse me, sir," Riley said. "I recognize that girl from a picture Kamuela once showed me. He really loved her." He walked to her.

Kimo's slap to his back distracted Spur for a moment. The smiling Hawaiian buck led a nude woman up the stairs to one of the bedrooms and some privacy.

McCoy stepped into the kitchen doorway, enjoying the spectacle of all that pent-up sexual energy being released at one time. It was amusing, and even erotic, but he wasn't in the mood for love-making. Celebrating, yes, but he had to catch his breath.

"Come on, Spur!" Jason yelled at him. "You gotta help me out. Missy here's not satisfied and I'm afraid I've run out of steam. Three times is my limit!"

"Yeah!" she said, sticking up her smiling face.

He smiled and shook his head.

CHAPTER THIRTEEN

At dawn, Spur woke in the bedroom he'd been assigned the night before he'd freed the Hawaiians. He yawned, splashed cold water on his face to fully rouse himself, and walked downstairs.

He stepped over snoring bodies and smiled at the exhausted remains of the all-out orgy. The men had mightily celebrated with their wives and sweethearts. They may not wake up for hours, but Spur had work to do.

He located Jason Miller and shook his bare shoulders.

"Hell, Missy, I can't do it again," he mumbled.

"Jason!"

Miller lifted his head and regarded Spur with sleepy eyes. "Huh?"

"You fully functional?"

He turned over and looked at his crotch. "I'm

swearing off women for at least a month, but other than that, yeah."

"Good. How much cash do you have here on hand?"

Jason scratched his stubbly chin and yawned. "I checked that last night. Found $2,000 in my father's safe. I remember him saying he was going to deposit it today."

"Think that'd be enough to get all these people back home?"

Another yawn. "Probably not."

"Then take that boat of yours, go into Portland and withdraw enough money to book passage for as many of the Hawaiians as want to go back, plus something for them to live on." Spur stooped, grabbed the man's hand and hauled him to his feet.

"Oh God!" Jason said, stumbling along behind him. He tripped over legs and feet.

In the kitchen, Spur sat the naked man in a chair and pumped water into the coffee pot. "How much are you willing to give the men for all the work they've done? How much to compensate them for their suffering?"

Jason Miller shrugged and yawned. "Hell, McCoy, I can't think straight now. Anyway, this chair's cold! Can't I just put on my britches?"

"No." Spur splashed him with water. "A cold butt'll wake you up. Whaddya say?"

"Uh, I don't know."

"Did your father ever tell you how much he'd made out here?"

Jason stifled a yawn. "No, but I looked at the ledger in his desk last night. Splash me again."

Spur dipped more water from the pot and sprinkled it over his shoulders.

"Shit, that's freezing. But it's working!" Jason shivered. "Okay. He had records of $20,000 in deposits."

Spur whistled. "Even if that's not all the money he made, that's enough." He did some rough calculations in his head as he set the coffee pot on the stove and opened the firebox. "Fifty into twenty-thousand," he mused, striking a match and setting the already-laid kindling alight. "Four-hundred dollars sounds about right."

"For each of them."

"Yeah."

"Including the widows?"

"Of course! And the bereaved sweethearts."

"Yeah. Fine with me." Jason violently shook his head and stared up at McCoy. "I don't want a cent of the money my father earned with human blood. I'll start all over, run this place like a real business. Advertise. All that shit."

Spur closed the stove door and turned back to the man.

"You were with Riley last night, weren't you?" McCoy nodded.

"He didn't give you any trouble?"

"No. Seemed to hate your father as much as you did. He warmed up to my side of the story real fast."

Jason sighed and rubbed his bare thighs. "Lay it on the table, McCoy. What happens to me? You gonna send me to jail?"

Spur paused. "If you pay the men the money and see that they get back to their home, nothin'll happen to you. I'll see to that. But Jason, if you try to pull anything on me you'll be behind bars so fast you'll—"

"Aw, come on, McCoy!" Jason shook his head.

"Trust me. I'm not my father."

"You sure aren't."

Kimo walked proudly back to Spur from the booking office, waving the tickets in his hands.

"Now I will see my six-year-old son," he said, his eyes shining. "Thanks to you."

The Hawaiian woman lowered her head. "We both thank you."

McCoy shrugged off their gratitude.

"I don't know how to—" Kimo lost his words in his throat.

"Look, just get on that boat, sail home and have lots more babies. Okay?"

The Hawaiian woman laughed.

"Forget about this place, Kimo. Put it out of your mind. You've got a family to think about now."

"I will. Thanks."

They shook hands.

Spur walked them to the dock where a great ship bobbed on the water. The brigantine *Flying Wheel* was leaving in an hour for Astoria. In ten days or so, weather permitting, the men and women would be back in Hawaii.

McCoy sighed as he walked to his room. His assignment with Harry Miller—now officially concluded after his testimony to Commissioner Golden and the telegram he'd sent to General Halleck—had been a break in his work to find the counterfeiters, but that job wasn't finished.

Yet.

As he made his way to the Riverside Hotel he passed the collection of cottages. The sign that bore Emily Curtis's flourishing autograph brought back the memory of the woman.

He stepped into her studio.

"Interruptions. Always interruptions!" the white-haired woman said before turning to him, brush in hand. Her lined face relaxed as she saw him. "Oh, Mr. McCoy." Her face sweetened with a smile. "How nice of you to drop by. Ah, I am rather busy right now." She gestured behind her.

Spur saw the young guard from Miller's logging camp standing uncomfortably on the platform. The stark naked youth gave Spur a lopsided grin.

"Hi."

"Hello, Riley." Spur couldn't hold back a laugh. "Picking up some extra money?"

"Yeah."

"You two know each other?" Emily Curtis asked.

"Ah, yes. It's hard to explain."

"I see."

"Do you have anything to tell me?"

She looked quizzically at him.

"Remember our conversation?"

"Landsakes! Of course I do. What do you think I am, a doddering old woman?"

"Never. Never!"

The aged artist turned back to Riley. "Put on your pants, young man, and wait. I'll pay you extra for waiting. And you, McCoy; come with me!"

He nodded and glanced at the canvas she'd been working on. So far the woman had captured Riley's thighs and everything that hung between them.

With a grin at the ex-guard, Spur followed Emily into a rear room in her studio. The air was heavy with the exotic combination of cigar smoke and lavender.

"I've been keeping my eyes open but I don't know much," she said. "Still, some of the egotistical bastards around here who think they have talent do some strange things."

"Like what?"

"You know, entertaining unusual visitors. People staying long hours, never seeming to leave."

Spur smiled. He guessed the obvious. "Customers, maybe? People buying paintings?"

Emily laughed. "Not those artless canvasses!"

"Models, then?"

"I don't know. Artists—even those just pretending to be true artists—are a strange breed. You'd never know it to look at me though, would you?" The white-haired woman stared defiantly at him.

"Ah, no. No I wouldn't, Emily."

She chuckled and patted his shoulder. "I'll let you know. You stop by anytime, young man!"

"Right."

Emily Curtis ushered him into the studio. "Okay, kid, take 'em off!" she yelled at Riley.

The man blushed.

Clare Maxwell slapped the money on the table. "Counterfeit! Fake! I couldn't believe it!"

"Where'd you get this?" Spur asked as he crossed his hotel room to look at the bills.

"Oh, ah, different places." She looked away from him. "You know, here and there."

Her evasiveness surprised him. When the woman had run into him on the street and demanded that he take her to his hotel, Spur had figured the pretty brunette had other things on her mind. Now this.

He studied the money. It was counterfeit, alright. No mistaking the slightly off-color ink, the smeared lower edge, the too-thin paper.

"I'm really nervous, Spur!" Clare said as he bent

over the table.

"About what?"

Though it was still daylight, he turned up the lamp to more brightly illuminate the bills.

"I feel like I can't trust anyone or accept any money. Sure, banks are supposed to be safe now, but anywhere else I'm bound to—to get more of this!"

"Hmmmm."

"It's getting so a girl can't—can't—oh, Spur, what can I do?"

"About what?"

"You know, money! That's $60 I've been cheated of!"

"I know."

"There's no way I can turn it in for the real thing?"

"No. Sorry, but that's impossible."

Clare frowned. "I knew it. So there's nothing I can do."

"You could always get out of the business," he gently suggested.

The woman blushed. "What—what business?"

"The kind of business where pretty young women make money, Clare."

"No. You have me all wrong. I've been a lot of things, but I've never been one of *those*!"

The look in her eyes beamed honesty. "Okay. Besides, most madames can spot a fake twenty. And they'd never pass it onto their girls unless they were real horrors."

He went to her. "Where'd you get this money?"

Clare squirmed and lowered her eyes.

He gently grabbed her wrist.

"Why's that so important to you?"

"Come on, Clare. I have to know. If you didn't want to talk about it, why'd you ask to come to my room?"

She stopped struggling againt his grip. "Because —because I didn't know where else to turn. I don't know anybody in this town." Clare pouted.

"Okay." He released her arm. "But I can't help you if you don't spill the beans." Spur sighed. "Is it something you're ashamed of?"

She lowered her head and nodded.

"And it doesn't have anything to do with sex?"

Her face colored and she stepped back. "No! Ah, not really."

Spur advanced to her. "So you didn't work in a house. You sold yourself on the street, right?"

"No!" Her voice was harsh.

"Then by god, Clare, what the hell did you do to get this money?"

"I—" She bit her tongue. "Oh Spur, I didn't know how I was going to live! I had to do something."

"What?"

"I dressed up like an old lady and went out on the streets."

"Go on." What was she driving at?

"I walked up to women and—and—" Again her voice faltered.

"And?"

"And robbed their purses." Clare looked away, seemingly very interested in the bevelled mirror that hung over the table holding a basin and pitcher.

He knew there was more. "That doesn't have anything to do with sex."

"I know." She bit her lower lip.

"What else, Clare? What else did you do to get all that counterfeit currency?"

"I—I—" She touched the left shoulder of her dress. "I took off my clothes."

Closer, he thought. "Why? I mean, was there someone else there?"

Clare nodded like a little girl who'd broken a dish.

"Who?"

She lowered her eyebrows. "Wait a minute. Wait a minute! You're awfully interested in all this, aren't you?"

"Yes." Okay, he'd tell her. "I'm a federal agent here in Portland investigating the counterfeit money."

She gasped. "You're—you're a policeman?"

"No. Not really. I only look into interstate crimes, especially those dealing with American money."

"Oh. Thank goodness! After I'd told you about my thievery I thought you might lock me up."

"Don't worry about that. I won't. Let's get back to the subject. Where did you take off your clothes?"

Clare frowned. "I did some modeling work the last two days."

That was it, Spur thought. "Who was this artist?"

"Alain DuLac."

CHAPTER FOURTEEN

"Heavens, Spur!" Clare Maxwell said as she stood before the man. "I wouldn't blame you if you booted me out of your hotel room for what I just told you."

He laughed. "Just because you posed as an artists's model? That's—well, that's art. Perfectly acceptable under the right circumstances."

The blush slowly faded from Clare's cheeks. "So I'm not a fallen woman?"

"From doing that? No." McCoy briefly smiled at the woman and peered at the counterfeit bills again. "But I wouldn't go back to that artist again if he slipped you phony money." He fingered it. "How many times did you pose for this man?"

"Twice. The first time he gave me one of those, but the second time it was real."

"Hmmmm."

"And I won't be going back to see him again. I

wouldn't even if he hadn't left the city for a few days."

"You said his name was DuLac?"

She nodded, her full attention to him.

"I recognize the name from the exhibit at the museum. He's gone out of town?"

"That's right. He told me when I left his studio two days ago. It didn't crush me. I wasn't counting the hours until I could humiliate myself in front of him again." She bent her head toward the floor. "At first I liked it, but then it just got so—so dirty. Seedy."

Spur went to her. "Clare, there's nothing humiliating about showing your body. Especially when it's a beautiful body like yours."

The woman lifted her chin and stared at him from lowered eyelashes. "Really?"

"Yes." The image of her standing there, defenseless in front of some aged European artist, was rather pathetic. "Was he any good?"

Clare lifted her eyebrows.

"I mean, does he have talent? At painting?"

"Oh, I'm no judge, but the picture did look like me—all of me."

"Maybe I'll see it for myself." Spur smiled reassuringly at the young woman.

She unconsciously licked her upper lip. "You mean the painting, or . . . me?"

Spur took a step toward her. "My dear Clare, I could never take advantage of a poor girl like you at a time like this." He unbuckled his belt, staring at her. She had all the signs. Clare was waiting for him, the woman with the arching brows and shiny cheeks.

"I suppose not."

She didn't retreat as he advanced on her. "Lost in this big city, low on money, barely recovered from doing something you detested doing just to buy a few crumbs to eat."

"Yes."

Spur slipped off his coat and let it fall to the floor. She raised her hands as he neared her. Nimble white fingers quickly clasped his shirt front, ripping off the buttons.

"It would be unthinkable to me to make advances on you, woman." He knocked off his hat.

"Of course!"

Clare's hands traveled from his now opened shirt down to his pants. Her eyes widened as she unbuttoned his fly, rubbing against the hardening lump with one palm. She smiled with delight at what she felt there between his legs and explored it, tracing its impressive outline.

McCoy rustled out of his shirt. "Miss Maxwell, you're safe with me."

Clare fumbled with his fly, furiously ripping away the cloth. "Uh-huh."

Spur watched her with amusement as her pink tongue darted between her lips as she worked on the simple task. When the last metal button was free, the woman reached inside and grasped his erection.

"Oh. Oh!" Clare looked up at him with a wicked smile. "Sure you won't change your mind? I'd like to be taken advantage of. Right here. Right now. Long and hard, as hard as you want!"

"Compromise your virtue?"

"Come on, Spur!" Clare stepped back and quickly undressed. Practiced hands removed the simple sheath from her body, exposing her creamy white chemise and cotton bloomers.

Spur readjusted his crotch. His stiff penis popped out of his drawers and reached for the ceiling. "You're forcing me into a difficult situation," he said with a faint smile.

"Difficult?" Clare said as she slipped the chemise off her head and lowered her bloomers. "It's the easiest thing in the world!" She glanced between his legs for the first time and sucked in her breath. "Come on, Spur. No more games." She panted and slid a hand between her thighs.

Spur rustled out of his boots, pants and long underwear and closed the drapes. In the semi-darkness, lit only by the single kerosene flame, he went to the woman.

Clare melted against him, kissing his shoulder, moving her lips across his bicep, tasting, clutching at his body like a drowning woman to a life raft.

Spur gripped the woman's buttocks and rubbed the soft cheeks. "You feel good," he said, pressing his throbbing erection against her stomach.

"You taste good." She flicked her tongue against his nipple.

"Two can play that game," Spur said as her teeth gently closed around the hard nub on his chest.

Clare laughed as he grabbed her head, pushed it back and bent before her. The woman's breasts hung there in a dazzling display of feminine beauty. He licked around her left areola, the warm flesh searing his tongue. Spur joined his hands behind her and forced Clare to arch her back, giving him easier access to her.

"Mmmm." He pushed her breast into his mouth, marveling at its firmness and size. It fit perfectly. Spur suckled her.

"Oh, you can compromise my virtue any day of the week."

As he worked her over Spur felt a hand worming between their bodies, grasping and squeezing his penis. Erotic waves of sensation flooded through his body. He switched to her other breast and gave it the full treatment—sucking, tonguing, nibbling, worshipping.

"I never thought I could want it this much." Clare's voice was breathy, dripping with tension.

He pulled off her with a loud smack. "Me neither." Spur put his hand between her legs and felt the furry patch. He slipped a finger into it, tracing her lips, teasing her as she teased him.

Their eyes suddenly met. The depth of the woman's expression increased Spur's desire. He probed her.

"Oh."

He pushed deeper. His fingertip touched her clitoris.

"Spur!"

Spur rubbed her, his hand splayed against her thighs.

"Stop it." Clare's voice was a moan. "Stop it! Spur, please!"

She circled her hips and pumped them up and down. He mercilessly aroused her, supporting the arching woman's back with one hand and torturing her with the other.

She squeezed her eyes shut and gasped, her hips jerking, her beautiful form tensing and releasing and spasming against his relentless finger.

For those few seconds he possessed her body, playing it like an instrument. Clare shook her head and straightened up. She locked her thighs around his hand.

"Hey!" Spur said, retrieving it.

"You don't play fair!"

"Who said anything about fairness?"

Clare's breath puffed out between her red lips. "You slimy bastard!"

Spur laughed in surprised delight as she threw her weight against him, sending him toppling onto the bed. The four-poster creaked. She scrambled around on top of him, jabbing her fingernails into his ribs, playing with his testicles, plunging her tongue into his ear.

The woman was all over him.

"Clare! Come on!"

She ignored him and lowered her head to his crotch. Spur's resistance melted away at the warm, liquid feeling of her tongue. She licked, outlining the flaring head of his penis, coating it with saliva.

His groin boiled with sexual energy. Spur slapped his forehead and raised his hips but she backed away, never quite taking him into her mouth.

"Damnit!" he said.

"Isn't that fair?"

Lick. Tease. Lick.

"That's enough!" Spur grabbed Clare's shoulders and rolled her onto her back. He parted her legs with his knees. The woman stared up at him with aware, aroused eyes.

"Okay—alright. Compromise my virtue!"

He grinned and pushed it into position. She was moist and more than ready. Spur sunk the first inch into her. Clare's face blossomed. She inhaled and nodded.

Spur drove into her body, sheathing himself until his testicles bounced against her. Their connection was so tight, so right, that they simply stared at each other in surprise for ten seconds, unmoving, reveling in the incredible desire building up in them.

"The—the—"

He kissed her. "No time for talk!"

Clare nodded. She rolled back her head as Spur withdrew and snapped it forward on his thrust. Her eyes tightened and he felt her body tense around him.

"Does it hurt?"

She nodded. "Yes. A bit. The boys back home are nothing like you."

He slowly pumped her. "I'll be gentle."

"No!" She flung the word at him. "Don't be! Just do it to me. With me!"

"Whatever you say."

Ignoring the sexual tension pulsating through him, Spur started slowly, gently pushing into her, sliding out almost all the way until she lifted her hips and demanded another penetration.

At first it was all he could do to keep himself from orgasming, but the hypnotic movements eventually allowed him better control.

"Yes."

Spur increased his pace, thrusting harder into her, faster, relishing the velvet feeling surrounding his erection. Their bodies locked together at the crotch.

"Faster."

He pushed into Clare with short, deep jabs. The woman smiled up at him, opened her lips and sank her fingernails into his back. Spur's pumps were so hard that the woman's body slid back and forth on the slick sheet beneath her.

"Harder!" she practically screamed.

Their pelvic bones banged together. Clare's breasts crushed against his hairy chest. She writhed beneath his body, fully enjoying Spur's rhythmic thrusts.

He suddenly lifted himself onto his hands and toes, riding her higher, changing his angle so that he rubbed against her clitoris. Clare went out of her mind, tearing her hair, her face suffused with the throes of the ultimate pleasure as he pounded into her body.

The old bed banged against the wall in time with Spur's movements. He slapped back down on top of her and pumped faster and faster. His throat tightened. The pressure built between his legs. Every muscle in his body tightened as he raced toward his pleasure. Clare's face below him dissolved into a soft, warm visage of ecstasy that gasped and moaned.

Beyond any semblance of rational thought, beyond all control, Spur thrust blindly into her, jerking and shivering and grunting as he drained his seed into her body. His wet lips molded to Clare's. His buttocks spasmodically humped between her thighs.

Time stood still. The moment stretched to infinity. Pump. Spurt. Thrust. Release!

Their mouths burned together, sealing their moment of love as he collapsed on top of her. Every nerve in his body flexed and finally quieted in the soundless wind of absolute peace.

Spur turned his head aside to take a breath and laid his cheek on hers. They stayed that way, joined together, spent and exhausted.

Finally, McCoy fought the lethargy leadening him

and raised his torso from hers. He stared down at the woman. Their lovemaking seemed to have magnified Clare's beauty—if that was possible.

"What . . . what happened?" she asked, lowering her eyebrows.

He managed a short laugh. "Huh?"

Clare looked up at him in surprised delight. "I mean—that only happens when I'm alone."

"Not when I'm around." He tenderly kissed her cheek. "I guess you don't have enough slimy bastards in your life."

She laughed and drew him into her arms, forcing him down on top of her again.

He gave her the tongue she wanted.

CHAPTER FIFTEEN

Clare turned to him as Spur finished dressing, smiling. She stretched like a cat and throatily laughed, shaking her head back and forth.

"What's that for?" he asked, buckling his belt.

"For the man who turned my day around. I came here mad and I'm leaving happy!"

McCoy shrugged. "No charge, ma'am."

She smirked, walked to the window and opened the curtain. Sunlight spilled inside, temporarily blinding Spur who backed to the bed. He tugged on his shoes.

"So this artist's name was DuLac?"

"Uh-huh." Clare put a hand to her mouth. "Spur! I just realized—that was my first time."

"Come on, Clare! You may not be a saloon girl, but I don't believe that."

She grinned. "That's not what I mean. I mean that

was my first time with a government man." She sat beside him and stroked his left thigh.

"Just don't go spreading that information around." Spur tied the laces. "Okay? I don't want anyone to know who I really am and what I'm doing here."

"Of course. I'll keep my mouth shut."

He kissed her as his left, booted foot hit the floor. "I hate to say this but—"

Clare pressed two fingers to his lips. "I know. I know. You have to go to work."

"Right." He kissed her hand. "As much as I'd like to spend the rest of the day with you."

"That's okay. I guess I'll live." She faked a swoon, falling into his lap.

Spur laughed as she picked herself up. He turned down the kerosene lamp and walked Clare to the door.

"If I get anymore of those counterfeit bills I'll tell you, Spur." She turned.

He grabbed her hand as she clasped it around the doorknob. "What kind of a man do you think I am?" he asked. "Where I come from a gentleman has the decency to walk a woman home after he compromises her."

Clare laughed as they left his hotel room.

Ten minutes later, the taste of her lips still lingered on his. He'd safely seen the comely woman to her hotel—a run-down but comfortable establishment close to the water. Interesting girl, Spur thought. With interesting information.

Time to return to work. He walked to the water-front colony and passed by each cottage until he found Alain DuLac's. It was easily identified by the huge sign that graced the front of the building.

The shades were closed. Spur walked onto the creaky porch and knocked. No answer. He tried the knob but it wouldn't move. The man had apparently left town just as he'd told Clare. He'd have to have a look around later that evening, when things were quiet.

Spur sighed as he walked around the side of DuLac's studio. All the windows were draped, blocking out prying eyes. He found one that was barely closed. He put his hands on his hips, bent forward and peered inside.

The sharp slap on his back made him spin around. "Mrs. Curtis!"

"I'm glad I found you." The white-haired artist smiled. "Come with me, young man. We can sit in my garden out back for a while."

"Why?"

"Just do it!"

Emily Curtis tugged on his coat sleeve so Spur gave in and followed her between the studios, walking past rhododendrons and azaleas just bursting into splashes of red and pink colors.

"I never could get just the right hue to capture those danged things," Emily said, pointing toward the flowers.

"You don't expect me to pose for you outside, do you?"

Emily laughed. "That's not what I want you for."

They entered a small, sparsely-planted garden.

"Please," the artist said, extending her hand to an iron chair.

Spur seated himself. The woman took up the chair beside it and gave him a wrinkled smile.

"Seen anything unusual?"

Emily Curtis leaned confidentially toward him.

"Yes. I mean, I have something unusual. Never trusted the man from the moment he walked into my shop. Putting on airs, talking up a storm."

"I'm sorry—" Spur began.

"*You're* sorry!" She coughed. "I'm out of cigar money for a whole month! That's what the man did to me!" Emily Curtis shook her head and slapped her thigh. "I knew it! Why don't I listen to myself? But I hadn't made a sale all day and the thought of making my rent overcame my better sense of judgment." She frowned. "I never should have taken it."

"Taken what?"

"Money. At least, I thought that's what it was, but it's not good for anything but cleaning off dirty brushes. A young fellow walked into my place yesterday afternoon and bought one of my paintings —a good rendition of Mount Hood in wintertime, with the sun gleaming on the snow pack." She frowned. "McCoy, I got cheated out of $60."

"I'm sorry, Emily." He reached for the woman's hand, but she pulled it back, stuffed it down her bodice and produced a slim cigar.

"You said you were wondering if any of these artists around here were into making this counterfeit stuff. Well, I don't know anything about that. And I'm sure I'll never see the man who gave it to me again."

"*If* he knew he was passing it to you, of course. But it seems there's quite a few folks in Portland who still don't look at their money."

"I know." She stuck the cigar into her mouth. "I guess I'm one of them."

Spur smiled at the comical sight of the elderly woman chewing on the stogie. "You don't still have this money, do you?"

Emily Curtis shook her head. "Nope. The bank took it from me."

He nodded. "Emily, your neighbor doesn't seem to be at home."

Her perfect white teeth clamped down on the end of the cigar, expertly severing it. She inelegantly spat it out. "That's right. Left yesterday afternoon."

"Did he say where he was going?"

"Nope." She examined the cigar. "But he sure seemed to be in a hurry. Only took one small bag with him. I heard through the grapevine that he's left Portland for a few days." She shook her head. "That's a strange one for you, that DuLac. Hey, Spur, got a light?"

Amused, Spur produced a match, struck it and held the flame to the tip of the cigar planted between Emily Curtis's lips. She puffed until it glowed.

"Thanks."

She worked it until it was steadily burning and blew out a mouthful of smoke. Spur thought. Alain DuLac had given Clare Maxwell a fake twenty, then left town. Maybe he'd gotten stuck with it and simply passed it on—knowingly or unknowingly— to the woman. Maybe DuLac was an uninvolved party in the transfer of the bill.

His leaving town seemed suspicious, but he'd invited Clare to come back for another session. It just didn't make sense.

Emily's loud exhalation brought Spur back to reality. "You really enjoy smoking?" Spur asked as a blue haze gathered around them in the garden.

She smiled broadly. "Sure. A woman can want a cigar just like a man, can't she?"

Spur nodded.

Emily puffed. "And they should have the right to do whatever they want to do. Period. My daddy taught me how to smoke when I was a little tyke. Course, that was after he'd caught me behind the barn, trying like mad to get the damned thing lit."

"I see." Spur rose and shook his head.

"I owe what I am today—this genteel, cultured, little old lady, to one man—my father." Emily winked at him, her head surrounded by a halo of smoke.

"Thanks for the talk, Emily."

"Sure. Any time!"

Spur watched the sunset, had dinner and walked to the Beacham Saloon. The drinking establishment was located just two blocks from the artists' studios. Might be good hunting grounds. He walked inside.

It was a dark, dirty place, smelling of smoke, liquor and cheap perfume. A smiling man plinked tunelessly on the piano. Soft-bodied, hard-eyed women paced up and down the place, offering their wares to a motley assortment of men.

Old-time sea captains tipped back glasses with fresh-faced sailors. Two bearded men exchanged short, volcanic bursts of dialogue in a foreign language, each banging on the table to make his point.

Many of the customers played cards. All of them drank.

"Try your luck?"

Spur looked down at the haggard man who shuffled cards on the table next to the entrance.

"Sorry, no."

"I'll guarantee you you'll win. I ain't never won fer as long as I've been playing." Nimble fingers fluttered the cards like a riverboat gambler.

"No money." Spur pushed through the tables and ordered a whiskey from the one-eyed bartender.

"What you starin' at?" the apron challenged him.

He hadn't been. "Nothing."

Sullenly, the barkeep exchanged the drink for Spur's money.

Every seat in the place was occupied so Spur moved to the rear and leaned against the wall. He slowly sipped the warm whiskey, staring, listening, learning.

Two men hunched over their cards on a nearby table. Their faces were hidden by their hats.

"Emily Curtis had three of 'em last night," one of them said.

"No shit!" His drinking partner whistled. "How the hell does she do it?"

"Beats me."

"Naw, that's what your wife does!"

Guffaws. A hand reached across the table and pushed the man's chest. "At least mine'll touch me, Sam!"

"With a ten foot pole."

"Just deal. You're drunk."

"Yeah. So're you."

The men fell silent and played poker. Spur turned away from them but looked back.

"Ole DuLac sure left in a hurry."

"Yeah, you hear about that?"

"Hear about what?"

"Come on, the dame! Seems his girl left him high and dry a few days ago."

"You mean that uppity slut?"

"Yeah. If she'd had any brains she would've stayed with him. He sure dressed her fine. Rebecca never had it so good on the street."

"Wonder why she ran off."

"From what I heard, seems she got tired of cleaning up after him. You know."

The speaker's head slanted upward, catching Spur's gaze. McCoy grunted and turned away. He sipped.

"Anyway, you know."

"Yeah."

Silence.

A pretty girl, about eighteen years old, waltzed through the tables to a silent tune, one hand held high, fluttering a lace handkerchief.

"Hey hey! A floor show and everything!" one of the men at the table said.

The man seated at the piano managed to find a genuine tune and stumbled through it.

The girl, her eyes dulled with alcohol and, probably, opium, grabbed the front of her dress and tugged on it.

"Hoowhee!"

"Yeah, Angel! Do it!"

The room burst with noise. Every man, including the bartender, turned toward the slowly circling girl, waiting, watching.

"Show us yer fine woman-flesh!"

Angel smirked and ripped her bodice.

Spur walked out of the bar. He wouldn't learn anything there that night.

The air was bitterly cold. Portland may be in for another taste of winter, he thought, buttoning up his coat. McCoy walked through the deserted streets until DuLac's studio was before him.

The windows were dark. Nothing seemed to have changed. Spur slipped to the back. The outline of a small door, painted a lighter hue of brown, showed faintly.

He opened his wallet and extracted the three master keys he'd received, compliments of the Secret Service. They were designed to open nearly every type of lock made and hadn't failed him yet.

The first one did it. Spur smiled and opened the door.

He banged his shins on something. He silently cursed and lit a match. The thin light showed that he'd entered a bedroom. He crossed it and went through another door into the studio itself.

Three easels were stacked like lumber against one wall. The match illuminated piles of canvases and stained boxes filled with tubes of paint. The flame singed his fingertips. He shook it out and lit another.

Spur moved silently through the large room. It was common knowledge that DuLac had left town so he couldn't risk lighting a lamp.

What was he looking for? Something. Anything that might pin the counterfeit money on the artist. It was all he had to go on so far.

Spur pushed into the studio, carefully avoiding the canvasses, the heavy furniture, the tables and chairs that littered the building like a maze.

He stopped to look at the painting that stood on a large easel, and was impressed by what he saw. DuLac was an accomplished artist despite Emily Curtis's harsh words. The half-finished bust showed wonderful talent.

It took him several seconds to realize that he recognized the woman. He bent toward it. It was

Clare Maxwell all right—from the waist up.

He buried the memories of their recent time together and turned from the painting. If I was a counterfeiter, McCoy thought, where would I hide the goods?

His boot came down on something that skittered across the floor. Spur bent, lowered the match and peered at it. Just a paintbrush.

It rested against the edge of a small rug that partly covered a dark stain on the floor. Spur shrugged, rose and put out the match before it burned him again.

He lit another and started to continue his search. For some reason, he returned to the spot, squatted and took a closer look.

He nudged the small rectangle of fabric away from the darkened area of the floorboards. The match didn't afford him much light so he held it directly against the stain, shielded his eyes from its glare and studied the spot.

The longer he looked, the more certain he was. The color was right. The reddish-brown stain wasn't paint—it was blood. Not more than a few days old.

Spur heard a cough as someone walked into the bedroom.

CHAPTER SIXTEEN

Spur dropped the match, suffocated it under his boot toe and silently walked to the front door. The unseen intruder moved into the studio.

"Alain! Are you in here? Why'd you leave the back door open?"

It was a woman.

"You always were touched in the head." She turned up the flame on a lamp. It revealed a pretty, very young woman wrapped in an overcoat. "You're not Alain!" Her eyes widened.

"No." Spur relaxed. "Who are you?"

"Rebecca Ledet. I used to live here." She looked around the studio. "You didn't do anything to Alain, did you?"

"No. I just got here. DuLac's out of town, from what I hear."

Rebecca shrugged. "Oh well, it's no business of

mine." She walked toward the bedroom. "I have to pick up a few things I left here the other day."

Spur followed the young woman. "You were DuLac's girlfriend?"

"Yes. What about it?" She turned up another flame and walked to the chest of drawers.

"You seem a little young."

Rebecca laughed and pulled open a drawer. "Young? Mister, I ain't been young since I was twelve—if you get my meaning." The girl rummaged through the drawer. "I know I left it here! It's my best."

"Did you know him long?"

"Who?" she asked with a sharp voice.

"Alain. Your last lover?"

"Long enough." Rebecca smiled and picked up a lacy petticoat. "Doesn't it just figure? Hidden beneath his long underwear. He always got mine mixed up with his." She folded the garment and looked at Spur. "You still haven't told me what you're doing here."

"No, I haven't." He leveled his gaze at the girl. Her face, free of makeup, was lovely.

"If you're planning to rob the place you'll be vastly disappointed." She smiled at her joke.

"That wasn't what I had in mind at all, but why say that? Alain DuLac is a fairly well known artist. I saw one of his paintings in the museum."

Rebecca's smile broadened. "That's called advertising. Alain figured it was worth the ten bucks it cost to have them hang one of his pieces of trash there. Don't you know anything about art?" She brightly blinked. "What else was I looking for? Oh, yes."

The girl knelt beside the bed, reached under the

quilts and tugged out a metal box. She flipped it open to reveal a mass of tangled chains, military medals, yellowing documents and a small leaden souvenir piece in the shape of Notre Dame. "I hate being back here, you know?" the girl asked him as she searched. "Even though he's not around I just hate it. Too many bad memories."

"You don't like him very much, I take it." Spur sat on the bed and stared down at her bonnet.

"I despise him!"

Maybe he could use it to his advantage. "I understand you helped Alain sometimes."

The girl grew still. She looked up at him. "What are you trying to say?"

"Did you?"

"You mean help him with love? Yeah, but he helped himself to that most of the time. That was just business between him and me."

"No, not that." Spur paused. "Come on."

Rebecca shook her head. "I don't know what you're talking about, mister." She continued pawing through DuLac's box of junk and memories. "Where is it? I know I put it in here for safe-keeping."

"Some boys down at Beacham's said you cleaned up after DuLac. I gathered they weren't talking about washing the supper dishes."

"Oh that," she said in a bored smile. "So?"

"Why don't you tell me about it, Miss Ledet? If that really is your last name."

She tilted her chin. "I'm of French extraction."

"Yeah, and I'm U.S. Grant! Don't change the subject, girl! What do you know about Alain DuLac?"

She sniffed. "You a policeman?"

Spur shook his head.

"Well, then . . . ah!" She lifted a glittering golden chain. A huge pendant, encrusted with rubies and diamonds, hung from it. "I got it!"

He tried a different approach. "What do you know about that stain out in the studio?"

"Oh, I don't know. Just a mess Alain made a few days back." She kissed the jewel, unfastened its clasp and hung it around her neck.

"You didn't do a very good job of cleaning it up," he observed.

Rebecca slipped the diadem into her dress.

Spur leaned toward the girl. "It's hard to get blood stains out when they have time to set."

"What makes you think I had anything to do with that?" She started to rise.

Spur grabbed her wrists and hauled her to her feet before him. "Look, girlie, I'm tired of this! Start answering questions."

"Get your filthy paws offa me!"

Rebecca struggled but she was no match for the brawny man. She gasped and twisted away from him, their arms interlaced over her head.

"Not until you cooperate!"

"Alright. Okay! Just let me go."

He released her. Rebecca Ledet stumbled away from him and rubbed her wrists.

"You sure don't know how to treat a lady."

"Show me one and I'll treat her. Come on. Who did he kill? And why?"

Rebecca shrank away from him. She started to speak, smiled and screamed shrilly.

A burly man raced into the room. "You let her alone!" the big-nosed thug said as he lunged at Spur.

He tried to side-step the man but a hand clasped his waist. Spur tumbled to the floor with him. He pounded his fist into the man's jaw once, twice, smashing it, sending him reeling back.

McCoy pushed the man off him, stood and drew his Colt. 45. A foot jabbed between his ankles and tangled up his legs. Before he could recover he was down again.

"Yeah, get him good, Ernie!" Rebecca shouted. "Kill the bastard!"

Spur's weapon slid across the wood. Furious, he laid a punch to the man's gut. The thug groaned and jabbed at Spur's face. A quick movement later and McCoy heard the satisfying crunch of the man's knuckles smashing into the floor.

He rolled out from under the man and looked around the room. Where was his revolver? Nowhere in sight. He glanced at Rebecca.

She smiled. "I'll never tell!"

Cursing, Spur stomped the kneeling man's chest, punching his torso backward. "I don't like the friends you keep," he said, shooting her a harsh look.

She crossed her arms. "Well, I don't like you. So we're even."

Blood oozed from Ernie's chin as he lumbered up. This was getting boring, Spur thought. The man ripped a long-bladed knife from his back pocket and slashed it through the air, daring Spur to come closer.

"Who's the big man now?" he said, and winced with pain.

The assailant slowly advanced on Spur, stalking, grinning. Spit oozed from his lips, turned pink on his chin and dripped onto the floor.

"Easy, easy boy. Don't wanna get that nice knife of yours all dirty, do you?" Spur asked.

"It'd be worth it," Ernie said.

Spur walked backwards. "Yeah. I'm sure Rebecca would clean it up for you." He bumped into something. A canvas crashed down. Spur moved past it and saw the glint of steel on the edge of the easel.

"Damnit!" Rebecca shouted.

Ernie's smile faded as Spur gripped the knife and swung it up. "Try it. Just try it!"

The big man spat. His face tensed. Spur ducked before the blade was out of Ernie's hand and heard it sailing over his head. The knife glanced off the rear wall.

Spur smiled as he rose. "You got a chance to make, Ernie. Die or get your ass outa here!"

"Damn you!"

"Is that trash wearing a dress worth it, Ernie? Are you really willing to give up your miserable life for that piece of filly meat?"

"Don't you call me that!" Rebecca said.

"Shut up, bitch!" he threw over his shoulder. "Your decision, Ernie. Your move."

He hesitated. His dumb face came alive—eyelids twitching, brows rising and falling, lips tightening into two white lines. He wiped the blood and drool from his chin and looked around the room.

The girl gasped. "Ernie, come on! Kill him!"

He stared at her. "I don't need you. Jesus, he's right! You're not worth it." The big man turned and walked out of the room.

"Come back and you'll get this buried in your chest!" Spur hurled the knife. Its blade dug into the wall and vibrated with a dull metallic sound.

"Well. You can't trust anyone!"

Spur strode over to the girl and shook her shoulders. "Talk. Now! Or I'll have you thrown in jail. Accessory to attempted murder."

Rebecca looked at him with dull eyes.

"You know what it's like in women's jails? Let me give you an idea. Four-hundred pound female guards with beards rule the roost. You'll be lapping between their legs on your first night!"

She recoiled from him. "Never!"

"Hey, after a coupla years, you'll get used to it."

"I'm only a little girl!" Rebecca shouted.

"Not since you were twelve."

She dropped her head.

"That's better. You have any more friends waiting outside for you to call them?"

Rebecca shook her head.

"Good. We're going to my place. And if you don't talk I'll drop you off at the police station. Come on!"

Rebecca didn't give him any trouble as they walked to the Riverside Hotel. After a few minutes she even started humming.

"What are you so happy about?" he asked, gripping her waist tighter to keep her from running off.

"I'm finally going to get back at Alain. If you can promise me I won't get into any trouble—"

"No promises," he said.

"Well, it's worth the risk. But I won't tell you here. How much farther is it? These shoes are killing my feet!"

"That's surprising. I figured you'd be used to walking the streets."

"Very funny."

She didn't give him any trouble on the way. Once inside his room, the door locked, the curtains drawn, Spur sat the girl in a chair.

"Okay!" Rebecca said. "So he killed a couple of men."

"How many?"

"I don't know. Two—three. Something like that. Maybe even four."

"How could you forget?"

"Wouldn't you try to forget about it?" She sighed. "I had some friends of mine—including Ernie—get rid of the bodies. Think they dumped them in the river."

That explains that, Spur thought, remembering his first visit with Commissioner Golden. "Why did he kill those men, Rebecca?"

"Oh, I don't know." She pushed a foot under her skirts and scratched her left ankle.

"What?"

She sighed. "Alain wasn't doing very well selling his paintings."

"Why did he kill them?"

The edge to Spur's voice made her sharply glance up at him.

"Tell me!"

Rebeccca fidgeted in the chair. She started to rise but Spur forced her back in her seat.

"So, because he wasn't making very much money with his artwork, he decided to go into a different business on the side."

"Counterfeiting?"

Rebecca looked up at him in surprise.

CHAPTER SEVENTEEN

"Counterfeiting? Heavens, what makes you say that?" Rebecca asked.

"It seems DuLac passed a phony twenty dollar bill to a friend of mine who did some modeling for him. I'm checking it out."

"So?" She shook her head. "That doesn't prove anything. Alain's so dumb he wouldn't know real money from the counterfeit stuff."

Spur just looked at the girl.

"But he thought he was smart enough to kill men for their wallets. That was his source of extra income." She faintly smiled. "Making fake money—that's beyond Alain's imagination. Or his talent."

Spur measured her. The girl sat comfortably on the chair, her face poised. Her breathing was regular and slow. Hell, he thought, she was such a cold turkey there's no way he could know if she was telling the truth. Her years on the street had taught her much.

"Look, I'm an agent of the federal government."

"So?" She glanced around the room, seemingly bored with the whole thing.

"Secret Service. I have the power to arrest and to kill in the line of duty. I'm here in town investigating the counterfeit money that's popping up all over Portland."

"Look, mister, I answered your stupid question. When are you gonna let me go?"

"What made Alain DuLac kill those men?"

"I told you," she said, her voice sharp. "He just wanted their money."

"What could drive him to kill for money?"

Rebecca shrugged. "I don't know. The man's crazy! He's out of his mind. All he ever talks about is Paris and how much he wants to go back there. I wouldn't mind going there to spit on his dead wife's grave. " She bit her lip. "That's all he used to talk about when I was still staying with him— Paris."

"So you didn't leave him out of shock when bodies started piling up in his studio. You left because you didn't like having to call your friends—like that perfect gentleman, Ernie—to dispose of the bodies. Right?"

Rebecca Ledet turned to him. "Mister, when you've been as down as I have for as long as I have, nothing shocks you anymore." Her face hardened. "I've sold myself more times than I can think. Smoked enough opium to put under ten Chinese men. I've lifted men's wallets to eat. I'm not happy with the way I've lived, but I'm still alive. When

Alain started killing every man who walked in here for who-knows-what-crazy-reason, I figured it was time to leave. So I did."

She wasn't a little girl. Rebecca looked years older than her tender age. As she sat silently before him Spur saw the lines creasing the corners of her eyes, the sad, worldly expression contorting her otherwise youthful face. Her hands were cracked and dry, her painted fingernails broken.

"Any more questions?" she asked.

He thought it over. Whether she knew anything or not, that was all he'd get from her. Might as well wait for the source, the man himself to return to town. Then he'd get at the bottom of this.

"You're quite a young woman, Rebecca—and I don't mean that as a compliment."

"I know, I know."

"Okay, Rebecca. Get back to whatever hole you crawled out of. But if you lied to me, sister, you will be behind bars. Got that?"

"Yeah," she said, tiredly nodding her head. "I got it."

Alain DuLac halted his carriage before the non-descript warehouse near the wharf. It was night-time, as usual. He didn't risk going there during broad daylight. He didn't wish to be connected with it just in case someone stumbled onto what he was doing there.

He tied up the horse's reins behind the building, unlocked the door and went inside. He'd been surprised how easy it had been to rent the space from a man who didn't ask questions and didn't want to answer any. DuLac simply paid his rent on time and that was that.

Now he lit the lanterns hanging along the far wall. The windowless building wouldn't reveal his presence inside. The artist ripped the dusty canvas off the printing press and calmly folded it up. Beside the press lay wooden crates. He smiled as he thought of how he'd secreted the counterfeit bills in the bottom of the crates so that they wouldn't be easily found. He'd been so careful, so very careful.

But things weren't working out like he'd planned. His short trip to Astoria had been disastrous. As hard as he tried, with as many connections as he had, he couldn't sell any of his counterfeit money. A few of the bills had shown up in Astoria and the alert was on. No one was buying.

It was time to shut down his operation in Portland, to move it somewhere else where he could unload as many of them in as quick a time as possible. A large city with lots of eager buyers.

San Francisco!

Now that Rebecca had left him there was no reason for him to stay in Portland. And maybe, in that art-conscious city, he'd sell his paintings faster than he had in the town on the Williamette River.

DuLac knelt on the cold floor and, with a prybar, opened a crate marked 'Made In Formosa'. He grabbed up the rubber-faced dolls and threw them behind him, quickly revealing the false bottom of the crate. He pulled up the thin piece of wood.

There they were. Neatly wrapped thousand-dollar stacks of counterfeit twenty-dollar bills. This crate alone—of the seven he had stashed in the warehouse—held $20,000. In the fresh market he should be able to turn it over for two of three thousand dollars. Alain DuLac smiled as he thought of his fortune there—soon he'd be $15,000 richer.

The image of Rebecca's face rose up before him, taunting him. DuLac stuffed the extra bills he hadn't sold in Astoria into the crate and refilled it with the dolls. He wouldn't be stupid enough to give his real money to some big-titted tramp again. No woman would get under his skin, would take control of him the way Rebecca had.

No more seventeen year-old girls with expensive tastes and exquisite bodies!

On his third consecutive night watching Alain DuLac's studio, Spur shrank back into the shadows as a drunken sailor and a woman waltzed by him on shaky feet, her giggles and his lewd comments slurred with the effects of too much alcohol.

DuLac hadn't returned home. After his night with the artist's ex-girlfriend Spur had thoroughly searched the man's studio but had found nothing—no counterfeit money, no plates, no printing press—to connect him with the scheme. He couldn't even find engravings of any kind.

Something about the way the girl had looked at him when he'd mentioned counterfeiting to her in his hotel room stuck in his mind. Though she hadn't told him anything he had this gut feeling. Spur followed it, sleeping during the day, staying up all night, waiting for the man to return.

Now, as a skinny dog padded by sniffing for food on the ground, Spur sighed and fingered his revolver. The tiny beast halted, pricked up its ears and barked at some imaginary enemy before scurrying out of sight.

A carriage approached. Its driver halted the four-wheel buggy before duLac's studio. The man's features were subdued by the thin moonlight but it certainly could be the artist, Spur thought.

The driver stepped onto the ground, brushed his hands on his thighs and walked to the studio's front door.

Spur slipped across the road and hid behind the carriage. He heard the squeak of the knob and the studio's door swinging open. McCoy moved past the horse and looked. The man was entering the studio. The agent raced across the ground and stepped onto the porch as the door closed.

Before the man could lock it, Spur forced open the door and walked in, pushing the astounded man to the floor.

"DuLac?" he asked.

"Ah, yes. I am Alain DuLac."

The room was even darker than it was outside, but Spur saw the thin outlines of the man sitting on his butt, staring up at him, the key still extended in his right hand.

"Where you been? Out on a little trip?" He snarled down at him.

"I do not have to tell you anything!" DuLac picked himself from the floor. He strode to the closest lamp and brightened its flame. "Who are you?"

Spur smirked as the light revealed the short, pudgy man. He drew his weapon and trained it on the artist's chest. "Come on, DuLac. Where's the counterfeit money?"

"What are you talking about?" he protested, unbuttoning his coat. "I am just returned from an exhausting trip and you accuse me of—"

"Ernie said I could get some from you."

DuLac froze. "Ernie?"

He'd caught the man off-guard. Good. "Yeah.

Ernie's a good friend of mine. Said you were an ornery bastard but that you had some quality merchandise."

DuLac shook his head. "If you come here to buy you do not show your weapon!"

McCoy laughed. "Ernie also told me how dangerous you are—how you don't mind stabbing your potential customers in the back."

The artist stiffened. "Ernie would not say that! Not about me!"

"He did—he even took me here to find you, but you were gone."

"Yes. I have business trip to Astoria."

"Forget all that. I want to buy. I wanna buy a lot. Where is it?"

"Do not rush me!" DuLac hissed. "I am tired. Very tired. You come back in the morning. Okay?"

As DuLac glanced at his easel, Spur was happy he'd returned the room to its normal appearance after his altercation with the bull named Ernie.

"Why are you still here? Leave!"

"I'll buy all of it—every bill you have."

Greed gleamed in the short man's eyes. "You are serious? All?"

Spur nodded.

He broke out into a sweat. "Well, I guess I could—" DuLac shook his head. "No. Come back tomorrow."

"Now! I'll give you cash money, DuLac." He patted his coat pocket with his left hand. "I have $5,000 waiting for you. You can't turn that down and you know it. And it's either tonight or you'll never see me again."

DuLac sweated. The breath blasted from between his lips. He thought it over, rubbing his chin, peering at McCoy.

"Well?" Spur demanded.

The man fidgeted with his coattails. "Okay. It is not here. You come with me."

"Sounds dandy to me."

They made a short carriage trip to the wharf. Spur wasn't surprised when the man led him to a small warehouse. It was perfect for that kind of operation—no direct, obvious connection with the counterfeiter. His idea to use Ernie's name had worked out fine. Now all he needed was the tangible, physical proof.

Like most criminals, DuLac couldn't turn down that much real money. His greed had overtaken his natural caution.

The immigrant artist let him into the building. As DuLac busily lit lanterns, Spur looked around the place. It smelled of mildew and dust, but fresh foot-prints marked someone's recent passage into the small warehouse. Canvas-covered objects littered the ground.

"Come on, DuLac! Stop stalling!" Spur said, snarling. "Where's the stuff?"

"Plenty of light. So you can see it."

McCoy grabbed his hand from the fourth lantern and jerked it away. "That's enough. Get it."

DuLac wrestled out of his fist. "Okay. Okay!"

Spur watched with interest as he ripped back a square of canvas. The man opened a wooden crate.

"Dolls?" he thundered. "You're trying to sell me cheap dolls?"

DuLac turned to him from where he knelt. "No. No! Wait a minute."

He emptied the crate and removed a false bottom. The artist produced a small paper-wrapped package and handed it to Spur. "Check the quality."

McCoy grunted and ripped off the covering. Inside it lay the counterfeit money. Crisp twenty-dollar bills. That was it. He had him.

"You make this stuff yourself?"

"Yes. Very good work, no?" The artist smiled up at him from the crate.

Spur nodded. "Not bad. I've seen better. Back in Chicago. By a man who used to work for the government. He's molding in a grave by now, six feet under." He felt the bill.

DuLac drummed his fingers on the wooden box, impatient. "You've looked long enough," he said. "It is fine. Pay me the agreed price."

McCoy snapped his fingers. "Sorry, DuLac. I just remembered something. I forgot to go the bank today."

The artist rose. "What did you say?"

"I don't have a dime on me."

Alain DuLac shook with fury. The soft lantern light showed the red that boiled up in his face. "You lie to me! You say you have money! Five-thousand dollars!"

"Hey, anyone can make a mistake."

Mistake!"

Spur smiled at the raging man. "I'll see you in the morning." He turned and looked over his shoulder.

DuLac scrambled across the warehouse floor. He reached under a piece of canvas.

"What's wrong, DuLac?"

"You die!" He hefted the revolver and fired.

CHAPTER EIGHTEEN

The lantern behind him exploded. Spur's shoulder hit the stone floor. He rolled as flaming drops of liquid and glass shards rained onto him from the bullet-ridden lamp.

"I kill you!" DuLac screamed.

McCoy came to a stop on his back. The small blaze that ignited in his crotch shocked him into action. He flipped over, smothered the kerosene-fueled fire against the floor, cursed and moved behind the heavy, canvas-covered object that had halted his dive to safety.

The artist stood in the middle of the warehouse, his weapon drawn, searching the shadows for his target.

Spur peeled off a shot. Expertly aimed, the bullet pierced the string attaching the lamp to the ceiling. The force of the lantern's impact as it hit the floor caused a spectacular explosion which consumed every drop of fuel. The fire burned itself out.

The light was much dimmer now. Good. Just the way Spur liked it.

"Where are you? Show yourself!" the artist raged.

He grinned. "It's over, DuLac. Drop your weapon or you're a dead man."

The immigrant wildly fired a second shot and scurried behind a stack of crates. "No. Not until you pay me!"

"You don't understand, do you? But then you're not from around here. I'm not buying your counterfeit money—I'm confiscating it for the U.S. Government."

Silence.

"Rebecca told me all about it, how you started printing cash instead of painting."

Spur heard the sharp intake of breath from across the room.

"No! That bitch!"

"We had a long talk last night—me and your girl." McCoy settled into his squat. "Hey, tell me something, DuLac. Is it true that your dick's only an inch long rock hard?"

The artist spluttered.

"Come on, DuLac. You can tell me. Just between us guys."

Feet scurried. He caught a glimpse of the man moving between two huge crates. The guy was trying to circle around behind him.

Two could play the game. Spur silently crossed the warehouse floor and slipped into DuLac's original position, crouching behind the crates.

Gunfire revealed the man's whereabouts.

"You moved!" the artist wailed.

"Ah, gee, I'm sorry about that, dickless!"

"You are a bastard!"

"And you're a criminal. You're also under arrest. Throw out your weapon. Now, DuLac!"

He roared and pounded four consecutive shots into the ceiling. A thick column of red brick dust poured down from it.

That's one way of using up your ammunition, Spur thought. "Come on. The game's over."

"No. No!"

DuLac moved too fast for Spur to properly target. He disappeared behind the huge object draped with canvas. The covering fluttered in the thin light.

"You're out of tricks, DuLac!" he yelled.

Two knives flashed toward him. Spur ducked as they slammed into the crate.

Shit! He had to admit the man was well prepared. Most criminals were.

McCoy shifted his position and peered around the blade-studded wooden box. DuLac wasn't in sight. He darted over to the next set of crates.

The canvas moved again. The artist must be searching for something.

"Why is that you men with little pricks won't give up, DuLac?"

"Shut your mouth!"

Their voices echoed in the warehouse.

More rustling.

What would it be this time now? A cannon? Spur smiled at the absurd thought until he saw the glow of a match.

No. The artist wasn't that prepared!

But he was unwilling to take the chance. Spur used the man's earlier trick. Crouching, he powered around the perimeter of the building, reaching the far wall and halted. DuLac wasn't in sight. McCoy snapped his eyes toward the door. Not there either.

Under the canvas? Yes. He'd probably lit the match for light.

Spur took a deep breath and walked up to it. "That's it, DuLac. Come on out."

A three-foot sword pierced the heavy material and jabbed at Spur's arm. It slashed back and forth, ripping the canvas. The artist blasted out agonized grunts.

"You could hurt someone with that thing."

"Damn you!"

"Trapped in your den like a wounded bear." Spur shook his head and stepped back.

The sword disappeared.

A tomahawk spun out of the huge tear and whirled inches from his head.

"Alright. I'll make you come out!"

The man was getting to him. McCoy was tired of him, tired of Portland, tired of the assignment. He stepped behind the huge object, away from the hole. The canvas draped out onto the floor all around it. What the hell was it covering?

Spur touched it with his left hand. The hard surface under the material seemed to be metal. An upright of some kind. He followed it down. It broadened into a flat surface.

It sure was heavy, he thought, as he pressed against it. The object barely moved. Then he knew.

Alain DuLac sprang from his canvas cave. He cut off his howl of delight—and removed his finger from the trigger—when he realized Spur wasn't in sight.

"Where are you?" he wailed.

Why not, he thought? It would do the job. DuLac stared stupidly away from him. Spur increased the pressure on the object, transferring its weight. It tilted.

The artist heard it and turned. "There you are!"

Spur groaned with the effort.

The Winchester's barrels went up.

The metal printing press tipped. Alain DuLac screamed as it toppled over. The tremendous weight pulverized him, smashing his body into a worthless pile of broken bones, flesh and tissue, crushing out his life.

The floor shook beneath Spur's boots for a second.

A gurgle. A sickening sigh. Then nothing.

Alain DuLac was dead.

Thomas Golden shook his head. "Not a pretty sight." He mopped his forehead with a handkerchief, stepped away from DuLac's lifeless body and looked at Spur.

"No, but don't complain. You won't find any more counterfeit money in your town."

The warehouse blazed with light. Policemen poked around. Some counted the money. Others were uncovering the astounding arsenal of weapons that the man had deposited throughout the small, mostly empty building.

The police commissioner shrugged. "I have to admit, I didn't think you had it in you, McCoy."

"Thanks for your vote of confidence in me, Golden."

"Hey, look this whole thing's been crawling up the back of my neck for weeks now. I wasn't thinking straight. Got all puffed up on myself."

"Guess so. Have your men crate up that counterfeit money. It's taking a train trip with me to Washington, D.C. The plates, too."

"Sure, sure, McCoy." He turned to chat with an officer.

Spur rubbed his neck. He was tired. DuLac's guts were starting to stink. "Get those men to move their asses, Golden!" he yelled.

The police commissioner smirked, stepped back and held out his hand. "After all, you're the highest authority here."

McCoy sighed. "Alright, you men! Move it! Get that money into those crates!" He walked among the uniformed officers who looked stonily at him.

"What the hell do you think this city's paying you for!" Spur bellowed. "Loafing? Hell no! I want those plates and every last bill of that counterfeit money at my feet in one minute! Move it!" The men hesitated, glanced at Golden and scrambled to fulfill Spur's order.

"Hey, not bad," the police commissioner said. "You ever thought about retiring from the Secret Service? This town could use a man like you."

Spur shook his head and walked into the sunlight.

"So I couldn't have done it without you, Clare."

Fresh from a bath and a shave, dressed in clean clothing, Spur felt like a new man. He sat in the restaurant across from the prettiest woman in San Francisco.

Clare pushed her hand onto his. "I'm flattered, but I didn't do anything!"

He gripped it. "Yes you did."

"Well, you did that too."

Spur smiled at her off-color joke. "Anyway, I'll

be leaving in an hour."

She sighed. "Sure. I know the kind. Love 'em and leave 'em. You men are all the same."

Then she smiled at him, the same smile he'd seen on DuLac's portrait. The smile of a confident, self-assured woman.

"Keep that up and you'll go far in this man's world, Clare Maxwell."

She tilted her chin. "Keep what up?"

"That. What you're doing just now." He squeezed her gloved hand.

Clare shook her head. "I've never been able to figure out what goes on in men's brains."

The waiter set two glasses of wine on the table.

"I take it you won't be posing anymore?" Spur asked after the man walked away.

Clare laughed. "I doubt it. That was my first and last adventure in that area. But I've been thinking. I'm already a fallen woman." She snickered. "So why don't I go all the way?"

"Now Clare, you don't have to do that! You've got so much going for you—you're intelligent, you're resourceful—"

"Honestly, Spur! Why are you always thinking I'm going to whoredom?"

Several other diners glanced their way. The noise level in the restaurant dropped considerably.

Clare smiled and lowered her voice. "No, no. I fooled people into thinking I was an old woman."

"Don't remind me."

She winced. "Sorry. Anyway, I heard about a theatre they have here. There's a new play opening up in a month."

"So?"

"So, I'm going to be an actress!" She lifted her

chin and gazed at the ceiling. The reflections of countless crystal lamps dazzled her eyes. "A great actress. I'll play the best female roles."

He touched her wrist, staring at her unbelievable beauty. "If anyone could do it, you could, Clare."

She lowered her eyes to his. "And I owe everything to you. My future's stretching in front of me like an empty stage. You've finally given me something to put on it!"

She bent toward him, kissed his cheek, moved back and raised her glass. "Know any good toasts, Spur?" Clare blinked her brimming eyes.

He nodded and clinked his goblet with hers. "To . . . art. Real art, not the counterfeit kind. May its world—the whole world—sing your praises, lovely lady."

They drank.